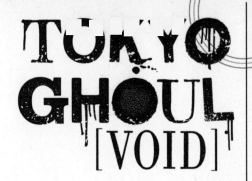

TOKYO GHOUL
[VOID]

SUI ISHIDA
SHIN TOWADA

TOKYO GHOUL-KUHAKU- © 2014 by Sui Ishida, Shin Towada
All rights reserved.
First published in Japan in 2014 by SHUEISHA Inc., Tokyo.
English translation rights arranged by SHUEISHA Inc.

DESIGN. Shawn Carrico

TRANSLATION. Morgan Giles with Kevin Frane

Library of Congress Cataloging-in-Publication Data

Names: Towada, Shin, author. | Ishida, Sui, creator. | Giles, Morgan,
   translator. | Frane, Kevin, translator.
Title: Tokyo ghoul: void / Sui Ishida, Shin Towada ; translated by Morgan
   Giles and Kevin Frane.
Other titles: Tåokyåo gåuru kåuhaku. English | Void
Description: San Francisco, CA : VIZ Media LLC, [2017] | Series: Tokyo ghoul
   ; 2
Identifiers: LCCN 2016047322 | ISBN 9781421590585 (paperback)
Subjects: | BISAC: FICTION / Media Tie-In.
Classification: LCC PL876.O78 T6713 2017 | DDC 895.63/6--dc23
LC record available at https://lccn.loc.gov/2016047322

Published by VIZ Media, LLC
P.O. Box 77010
San Francisco, CA 94107

Printed in the U.S.A.

10 9 8 7 6 5 4 3 2 1
First printing, January 2017

VIZ SIGNATURE
www.viz.com

東京

TOKYO GHOUL

TOKYO G GHOUL

東京

SUI
ISHIDA

T O K Y O G H O U L
[V O I D]

喰種

Novel

[VOID]

ORIGINAL STORY BY

**sui
ishida**

WRITTEN BY

SHIN
TOWADA

TRANSLATED BY
Morgan Giles
with Kevin Frane

cast of characters

KEN KANEKI

A boy who received an organ transplant from a Ghoul. Now a person who eats people. That conflict and difficulty will change his fate.

KOTARO AMON

A Ghoul investigator fighting every day to protect humans from Ghouls and correct the order of the world. Has had a close connection with Ghouls since his days in the orphanage.

KYOHEI MORIMINE

A police lieutenant in the 8th Ward. Investigating a case of a missing schoolgirl.

KOHARU UTSUMI

A graceful girl who knows Amon. Seems like she might be caught up in some kind of trouble.

ASA

Ghoul. Looks like a delinquent boy but is actually a girl. Wants to be a mask maker like Uta.

UTA

A Ghoul who runs a mask store in the 4th Ward. Used to clash with Yomo, but they've reconciled now.

TSUMUGI YAMAGATA

A human who makes masks so beautiful they took Asa by surprise. Also on friendly terms with Uta.

SHU TSUKIYAMA

Ghoul. Considers himself a "gourmet." Now has quite an attachment to Kaneki.

CHIE HORI

Tsukiyama's friend from school. Wanders around taking photos.

IKUMA MOMOCHI

A Ghoul who came to Tokyo from the countryside. Wants to be a musician.

MITSUBA

College student, idol singer. Not very assertive. Even her fans aren't sure why she became a singer.

TOUKA KIRISHIMA

A female Ghoul. Nicknamed "the Rabbit" by the CCG and considered dangerous. Goes to school and has human friends.

HINAMI FUEGUCHI

A female Ghoul whose parents were killed by Ghoul investigators. Part of Kaneki's group.

KAZUICHI BANJO

Former leader of 11th Ward who was in love with Rize. Weak. Part of Kaneki's group.

MISATO GORI

A Ghoul investigator affiliated with the 13th Ward. Has developed an interest in Amon...

IWAO KUROIWA

A special class Ghoul investigator. Nicknamed "Iwaccho" by Shinohara. Strong as an ox when he fights.

東
京
喰
種

TOKYO GHOUL

[VOID]

種

TABLE OF CONTENTS

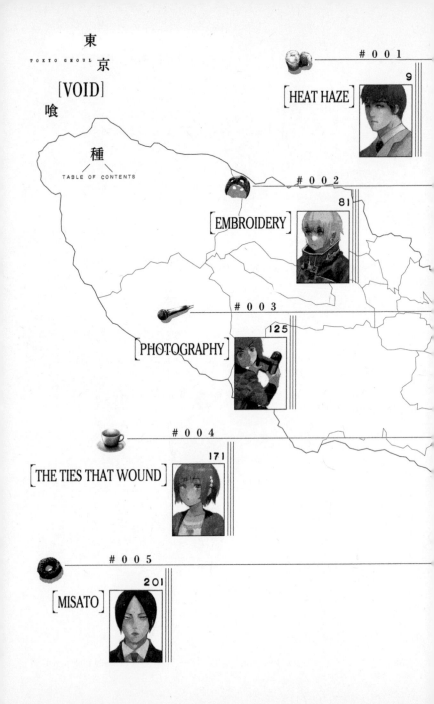

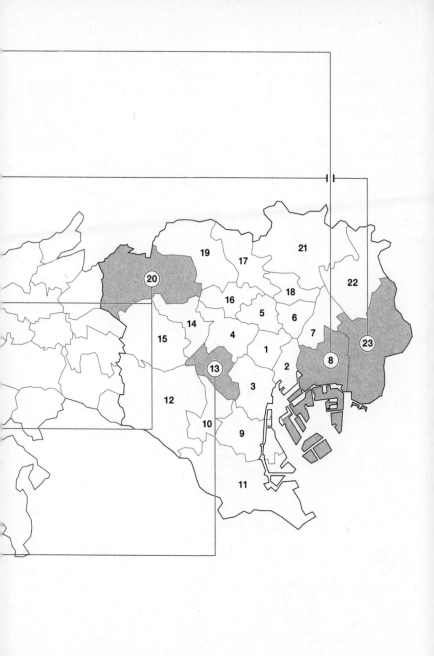

東京 — [VOID] — 喰 種

On the other side of the wall of my unshakable beliefs there is, perhaps, a whole world I don't know.

"You want me as a reinforcement for the 8th Ward?" Amon said, echoing the other man's words without realizing he was doing it. The afternoon sun pierced the thin lace curtains in the hospital room. Kotaro Amon sat on a stool with his back to the window, and his eyes were wide with surprise.

Lying in the hospital bed was Amon's boss, Yukinori Shinohara. His nickname was the Indomitable Shinohara, but looking at him now, he was so covered in casts, bandages, and bruises that it was more difficult to find part of him that wasn't injured in some way.

"Yeah," grunted Shinohara. "At the moment we've got a serious shortage of talent, as I'm sure you know, but the 23rd Ward is the worst off of all. During the attack on Cochlea, investigators from the 23rd Ward were the ones on the front lines. But they didn't stand a goddamn chance against a bunch of organized Ghouls."

Ghouls—an absolute evil infesting this world. These repulsive creatures look just like humans, but prey upon them. Their bloodlust leads them to kill innocent people and feast on their flesh.

And we, the group of professionals sworn to destroy them, are known as the Commission of Counter Ghoul—or the CCG for short.

Amon was part of the CCG elite. He had graduated top of his class at the Academy, became skilled in the use of Quinques—a weapon developed to battle Ghouls—and now, as a Ghoul investigator, he battled Ghouls daily.

His efforts had been recognized just a few weeks earlier as a result of his involvement in the search-and-destroy operation at the 11th Ward headquarters of the Aogiri Tree, the Ghoul organization dedicated to terrorizing CCG investigators.

It was impossible to get a full picture of these Ghoul organizations. And that problem, combined with the sudden reappearance of the mysterious monster known as the Owl, who had done catastrophic damage to the CCG a decade prior, meant that the battle was fierce.

And then those of us who went in there and saw good men sacrificed in the name of defeating Aogiri barely got to soak in the afterglow of victory, because suddenly we were informed that there had been an attack on Cochlea, the Ghoul detention center in the 23rd Ward.

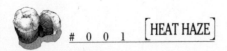

0 0 1 ⎡HEAT HAZE⎤

The Aogiri Tree's aim from the beginning had been to free the Ghouls imprisoned in Cochlea. Ghouls who investigators had struggled to catch were suddenly unleashed onto the streets, and the CCG was still searching for some of them to this day. Who knew what kind of new atrocities would be committed if they didn't quickly redress the issue?

"Now, headquarters is investing as many elite officers as it can get in the 23rd Ward... but there just aren't enough men to defend the surrounding wards. So, as the 8th Ward is one of those surrounding wards, that's why I want you to provide some assistance there."

"I see... But sir, as you know, I am currently without a partner. Do you really think it's safe for me to go into this alone?"

Since losing Kureo Mado, the first class Ghoul investigator who had taken him under his wing when Amon was a rookie, Amon had gone without a partner.

But now Shinohara, who had been looking after Amon as a protective measure until a new partner was found for him, had been injured in the battle against Aogiri, making this a painful time to be changing duties.

"Look, after this incident, everyone knows what a strong fighter you are, and in any case, they're really shorthanded. I don't have any control over this. Anyway, this is just an interim measure for a month or two until they appoint a successor for the 8th Ward."

"Right... I see. I'll still be worried about the 20th Ward, but I'll work hard to be strong for the 8th Ward," Amon said.

"They're counting on you. You'll be lightening the workload for the guys in the 8th Ward. The number of complaints I hear from them makes my head hurt."

"Complaints?"

"Just about how tough everything is," Shinohara said.

They exchanged one or two more comments, but feeling that hanging around Shinohara's room would only slow his healing, Amon soon left.

The hallway outside was busy with nurses coming and going. Amon stood there in the hall for a moment, the sound of their footsteps in his ears, as he looked down over the city from a window. His eyes slid down to the people walking along the tree-lined street next to the hospital. Amon stared out at them.

That eye patch . . .

The sounds of the hospital fell away into the background. Suddenly his mind was plunged back into the events of the Aogiri offensive. During the battle, when he'd been looking through a broken window frame, he'd seen someone wearing an eye patch. And that enemy had escaped him.

When the memory of the eye patch came to him, it was like he was taken back to that day.

The feeling of hatred was so distinct, and yet the memory was like a heat haze.

Kotaro . . .

And the Ghoul who had raised Amon as if he were his own child still haunted his memory, too.

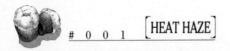

\# 0 0 1 [HEAT HAZE]

II

Early the next morning, attaché case in hand, Amon arrived at the train station nearest to the 8th Ward. The 8th Ward was in a coastal area, and often, depending on the direction of the wind, you could smell the sea.

Part of the swell of commuters and kids on their way to school, Amon had stopped to look at the map outside the station to find the 8th Ward branch when he heard a voice ask, "Are you trying to get somewhere?" He turned to find a sophisticated-looking woman standing next to him. She looked to be about the same age as Amon.

Beside her stood an elderly woman, probably her mother. She looked around nervously, as if she were afraid of something.

"Oh, uh, the local CCG branch office..."

"You want to go three streets down and turn onto the main road. Just go straight and you really can't miss it. Look, it's right there. When you see the bookstore on the corner, that's where you turn."

"I see, so that's where it is. Thank you for your help."

Amon walked the way that she'd told him to, and soon he saw the 8th Ward branch office. He adjusted his tie and went through the automatic doors. At reception he gave his name and said that he was sent as reinforcement; he was shown to a conference room where he waited nearly five minutes before two men in suits appeared.

"Amon, sorry for dragging you all the way out to the Eighth."

"Yanagi, are you running the show here now?"

Yanagi held out his hand first for a handshake. He had few stand-out achievements, but he was very flexible and his work was solid and dependable, so he was often sent to fill a gap in districts that needed help badly. Amon had met him several times in the past.

"After the Cochlea incident, we were sent here to take charge. I mean, I've worked here a few times in the past, so I don't mind."

So he's just filling in this time too. But why is Yanagi here to welcome me instead of someone actually based in the 8th Ward? Are things really that dysfunctional here?

"Mr. Amon! We've heard a lot about your performance in the Aogiri battle! No surprise from the guy at the top of his class at the Academy," said the other man, Tojo, who was Yanagi's subordinate.

Tojo had more seniority than Amon, but the bright, chatty man was still a second class investigator. Because of this, he always addressed Amon politely. Amon wished he would just speak to him normally, without worrying about rank and all of that, but every time he told Tojo this, the man answered, "But what's wrong

0 0 1 [HEAT HAZE]

with being polite?"

"No, man . . . When I saw how all the top-ranked investigators fought in the Aogiri operation, all I could think about were my own shortcomings. I still feel like that," Amon said.

"Oh? But how amazing it must be just to be able to say you were there. I mean, that's the real front line for the CCG. Tell me, were there guys using really rare Quinques? Oh, and what's Juzo Suzuya like? A guy like that who's only rank 3 but still gets to—"

"That's enough," said Yanagi, cutting off Tojo's uncontrollable torrent of questions. Glaring at Tojo, who took a step back as if he were going to run away, Yanagi put the file he'd been carrying down on the table.

The first page was a map of the district.

"You might have guessed already, given that we've drafted you in as reinforcement when we were just brought in ourselves, but at the moment we are the only investigators on the beat in the 8th Ward."

So my bad premonition was right. Damn. Yanagi's expression was severe.

"Some of the escaped Ghouls from the 23rd Ward fed on people on their way through the 8th Ward, and when one tried to escape, it turned into a battle. Lots of casualties."

Yanagi stabbed the map with his finger, pointing to the 8th Ward. "The fugitive was a rate A Ghoul. Not especially strong. But unluckily enough, there was not one investigator from the bureau in the ward. I know I shouldn't be saying this, and I might be criticized for it, but most of the best investigators were taken from us in the Aogiri incident . . ."

When Amon himself had seen the selection list for the current 11th Ward Special Countermeasures Team, he had been concerned about how thin investigators were on the ground in the areas surrounding the 23rd Ward. The 20th Ward, where Amon had been based, was a designated danger zone, so officers like Hoji and Takizawa were on call, but the 8th Ward wasn't so designated. It was a place that had always had fewer investigators.

"What happened to the Ghoul?"

"We got him and sent him back to Cochlea."

"You guys did?"

Yanagi and Tojo nodded in unison.

"As I said, this is not the first time I've worked in the 8th Ward," Yanagi said. "When I heard about the Cochlea attack, I immediately worried that the escaped Ghouls would flood into the 8th since it neighbors the 23rd Ward, so I came back."

"Well, that and we were ordered to report here by the bureau."

"They were sending the toughest guys here, so they sent us. In my opinion, anyway. So at any rate, I got a call from a guy I used to work with, a clerical investigator in the 8th Ward, saying that Ghouls were creating mayhem here. And then, when he rushed to the scene of the crime . . . he was eaten."

Yanagi bit his lip as memories of the tragedy came back to him.

"So after that, we were put in charge of the 8th Ward here. The three wards adjacent to the 23rd Ward are the 22nd, the 7th, and this one. And after the Cochlea attack, another high-ranked investigator

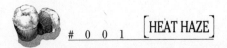

was killed in the 22nd Ward, where masses of escapees have apparently flooded in. The 7th Ward has always had a lot of investigators assigned to it since there's a restaurant there that's rumored to be a meeting place for Ghouls. And yet, here . . ."

Tojo shook his fist. "I told them from the beginning to send more high-level investigators to the 8th Ward, but after we captured and got rid of those Ghouls they just abandoned us because they said there had been no fugitive-related incidents! So that's why, even though the 8th Ward borders the 23rd, it's just me and Yanagi here. What a catastrophic mess—Agh!"

Tojo's rant ended with a cry, due to the hard thump Yanagi gave him on his head.

"Ahem. To get back to what we were talking about, Amon, this time there was a big incident with some rate SS monsters that got away. Now there are frequent incidents centered on the 23rd Ward, and we think these escapees are the cause. But still, the 8th Ward is a lower priority than the others. Whatever we do, we gotta do it ourselves."

That was the problem that had been imposed on Yanagi and Tojo: figuring out how to protect the residents of the 8th Ward with very few men. Now Amon more than understood the issues in the Eighth. "So what should we do?" he asked.

"Today, first, we'll take you around the ward. After that, we want you to be vigilant about the 23rd Ward and strive to maintain security. We've had to put the search for suspected Ghouls on the back burner, and repairs to Cochlea after the attack are still incomplete.

Anything could happen."

"Got it. You can count on me."

"Right, let's head out," Yanagi said.

The three of them finished getting ready, left the conference room, and got on the elevator. Suddenly, Yanagi's face softened slightly.

"Amon, we really appreciate you coming here. As I said before, we lost a lot of investigators who had been working in the 8th Ward. Work has come to a standstill, and we're getting a lot of grief from certain quarters."

"Certain quarters? Do you mean the bureau?"

"No, no, not that."

The elevator arrived at the ground floor, and as they headed out into the lobby, Yanagi shook his head. "Investigators like us need cooperation from people in a broad range of industries, and their businesses are being hit hard. The thing that's worrying me most right now is . . ."

Yanagi sounded weary and Amon wondered, as he listened, what exactly had happened here. But before Yanagi could tell him, a voice cut in.

"That's what I keep telling you! Why the hell do I have to meet with you at your convenience?!"

The man's voice echoed through the lobby. Yanagi and Tojo stopped, almost robotically, but Amon headed toward the shouting, wondering what was going on.

"Sir, as I said the other day—"

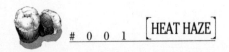 # 0 0 1 [HEAT HAZE]

"Because you guys can't get it together to put out the results of your investigation, I can't do shit! Give me a break here!"

Amon saw a man getting violently angry with the receptionist.

"What's he doing..."

He was in his mid-thirties, wearing a worn suit and an untucked button-down shirt. He banged his fists on the desk as he cursed at the receptionist.

That's enough of that. Amon's strong sense of responsibility took over. He strode toward reception.

"Hey, Amon, wait!"

Ignoring Yanagi, he stepped in between the man and the receptionist.

"Huh? Who the hell are you?" The man plunged his hands into his pockets and glared at Amon.

"What's all this trouble you're causing the receptionist?"

"I'm the one getting troubled here. Outta my way, I'm getting this settled today." Many men might hesitate when faced with a tall, stocky man like Amon, but this man was unfazed.

"If you cannot have a rational conversation, I will call security."

"What is this shit?"

"I will call security, I said. So, shall I?"

The man snorted. *Seems like he doesn't want to listen to what I have to say*, Amon thought. *If he thinks he can brush me aside like that I'll give him something to really be angry about.*

"Amon, cool it! He's..."

Before Yanagi, who was rushing forward, could finish his

sentence, the man took something out of the inner pocket of the jacket of his worn suit and held it in front of Amon's face.

". . . a police officer."

The man held up his badge to show Amon. On it was a photo of the man clad in a uniform with his rank and name—Kyohei Morimine—printed beneath.

"Y-you're a cop . . . ?"

"If anyone's getting restrained around here I'm the one doing it, okay?"

He put his badge back where it came from and stared at Amon with a look of appraisal. "You look like a friend of Yanagi and Tojo's. So you're a Ghoul investigator too, huh? Hmm . . ."

Yanagi, who had tried to stop Amon, and Tojo, who could only look on not knowing what to do, both had looks on their faces that spelled out what a huge mistake Amon had made.

"Well, I might have been a little . . . rough with you earlier. I apologize. Sorry. And miss, I'm very sorry to you, too."

The man somehow maintained his terribly pompous attitude even as he apologized. He looked at Yanagi and grinned.

"Hey, Yanagi, you know, I'm pretty sure you said, 'If we just had one more guy we could start investigating again.' "

"He just got here today, Morimine . . ."

"A promise is a promise! See, it was worth it coming down here every day. Hey, new guy, can I count on your cooperation?"

"Cooperation?" Amon could not understand what he meant, so he turned to Yanagi in search of an explanation. Yanagi furrowed his

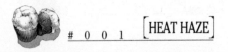

0 0 1 [HEAT HAZE]

brow and scratched his head.

"Well, Amon... this is Lieutenant Kyohei Morimine of the 8th Ward Police Station, Criminal Division. He's a very talented detective, however you slice it."

"Nice to meet you," Morimine said, changing his attitude completely. He snapped to attention and gave a salute. *Sure does seem like a cop.*

"Morimine, this is Kotaro Amon, who has come from the 20th Ward as an urgent reinforcement. He's young, but he's a first class investigator."

"Oh? He couldn't be younger than Tojo here, could he? And he's a first class investigator?"

"Cut it out!" Tojo said. "That's a delicate subject and you know it."

"Tojo, what's your rank again? Rank 2, was it?"

"Man, I told you, cut it out!"

"But he's younger than Tojo here, right? And isn't first class higher than rank 2?"

"Of course it is, you bastard! Agh!" Yanagi silenced Tojo's yelling with another thump.

Amon, still puzzled, finished the formalities. "That's right, I'm Kotaro Amon," he said.

"But... what is a detective doing here?"

I'm still not sure I believe he's a cop, but we can't get started if we don't listen to him.

"I'm here about the missing schoolgirl case from three months

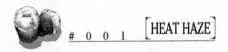

0 0 1 [HEAT HAZE]

ago," Morimine said.

"A missing schoolgirl? You don't think it's got something to do with Ghouls, do you?" Amon asked Yanagi, who was standing beside him, but Morimine answered instead.

"Hell no!" he scoffed. "Definitely the work of a human. But the higher-ups made a big fuss at the first sign of Ghoul involvement, and they gave all authority to the CCG. And then if there's a danger of Ghoul involvement you have to follow all these tedious regulations, so I can't even investigate freely!" Morimine started rattling through his list of complaints.

"Calm down a little, Morimine," Yanagi warned and began to carefully explain. "Three months ago a schoolgirl went missing and the police started investigating, but last month a barrette belonging to Mai Hirano, the girl who had gone missing, was found. And where the barrette was found there was also some bodily fluid thought to be from a Ghoul. So we received a request for cooperation from the police . . ."

"'But all the chief investigators are in the hospital, and it doesn't look like we'll be able to resume the investigation!'"

Now Amon understood at last that due to the personnel shortage after the Aogiri incident, they hadn't been able to assist with the case's investigation.

"I know you guys are out there putting your lives on the line for us, but we're doing the same thing! And we cannot afford to neglect this forever!" Morimine crossed his arms and stared at the three of them. "Yanagi, did you get a match on that bodily fluid?"

"Unfortunately this was the first time the CCG has 'met' this particular Ghoul."

If the Ghoul had attacked people before, and if the victims' remains were passed on to the CCG for investigation, then the details regarding the fluids left on the corpse—as well as the Kagune marks, if any—would be recorded and registered under a unique Ghoul ID number. If information was immediately collected when a new incident was uncovered, it greatly aided investigations, but in this particular case it seemed like the culprit had been a new Ghoul. That meant the investigation had to start from the very beginning.

"So what's the possibility that this Ghoul suspect was actually involved in the case?"

The CCG knew of some Ghouls who always marked their territory. *If we can find out which one of them was involved in this, it might eventually lead to the extermination of Ghouls.*

"Just when they were in the middle of figuring out the answer to that question, the investigators were injured and had to be hospitalized."

"I see . . . so nothing's been done. Or to put it in other words—we are not currently disclosing information relating to this case."

Both the police and the CCG were sworn to protect the peace, but their approaches differed significantly.

Particularly, when dealing with the special field of Ghouls, the CCG imposed confidentiality regarding the specifics and limited the information provided to outside agencies. They could not simply pass on information about a Ghoul suspect and let the police

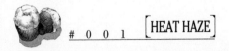

[HEAT HAZE]

investigate. Which had led to Morimine's frustration.

"Since the possibility emerged that the culprit might be a Ghoul, we've moved carefully," said Morimine. "But you guys haven't touched the case. The missing girl might still be somewhere waiting for someone to save her! If you're not going to do anything then give the case back to us!"

"Morimine, we're doing all we can, but until we determine there's no chance a Ghoul was involved we can't release the case," Yanagi said.

"Oh, I've heard that one before! Don't even bother. You said it, Yanagi—you said that as soon as you got another Ghoul investigator on board you'd be able to start on the case. Didn't you?" Morimine got in Yanagi's face as he carried out his interrogation. Yanagi looked like he was at his wit's end. He pushed Morimine away from him with both hands.

"I have a wife and kids too, Morimine. What happened to this girl is breaking my heart, even if there's no connection to Ghouls. Of course I want to investigate. But Amon here just got to this branch today. I want a little more time to get the 8th Ward under control first," said Yanagi.

"I've waited long enough already! I want you to get started right away. And I'm not leaving until you do!" Morimine's eyes cut straight through Yanagi, then Amon.

"Understood."

Now Amon looked at Yanagi and Morimine.

"'Understood?' Amon?"

"Chief Yanagi, I'm going to investigate this case."

The pounding in my chest stopped for a moment, until he started yelling again.

"All right! Don't go back on your word!"

"H-hang on a minute, now, Amon..."

"No, no, no, no, no, Amon! Amon!"

Morimine was exultant, but Yanagi and Tojo's expressions had changed. They grabbed Amon by the arms and pulled him away from the lieutenant.

"I think it would be better for us to handle such sober and... unglamorous work. Agh!" Yanagi hit Tojo again, but he seemed to be in agreement with Tojo.

"Amon, you'd be the right man for any job. And once we've finished briefing you on the 8th Ward, we'll start working on the case. But your job, for now, is being vigilant as regards the 23rd Ward and maintaining the security of the 8th..."

But Amon said, "No. I still don't know that much about the 8th. And since the threat from the 23rd requires serious attention, I think you and Tojo are much better suited to that, given your ability to see the 8th Ward from a much broader perspective."

"Amon..."

"The search for this Ghoul suspect will take me all over the ward, so I'll be able to get the lay of the land while I'm doing it. And if there's any chance a Ghoul was even slightly connected to this case, we can't just put it on the back burner."

Amon's sense of pride would not allow the CCG to be

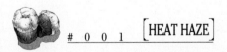

0 0 1 [HEAT HAZE]

condemned unfairly by the police due to circumstances beyond the control of investigators like himself, who were fighting every day to serve people and protect the peace.

A dark look passed over Yanagi's face, but he nodded in agreement with Amon.

"So, Morimine, are you gonna give him the information and time he needs to take over the case?" asked Yanagi.

Morimine put his thumb and index fingers together, giving him the OK sign.

III

After a quick information handover was completed, Amon left Yanagi and Tojo, who seemed somewhat worried, and headed toward the train station. One of the Ghoul suspects on their list lived in an apartment near the station.

Lieutenant Morimine walked alongside him.

"Should I send my report on the investigation to the police station when I'm done?"

"You really are new to this ward, aren't you? You gotta get a map or something. By the way, that's the way to the train station."

Morimine pointed at a narrow side street between two buildings. *How did he know I was heading to the train station?* Amon realized Morimine had been peeking at the document he was holding and felt his mood take a turn for the worse.

And Morimine felt the change. "I wasn't looking at that," he said. "I figured you were going somewhere you knew, because you came out of the CCG building and went right off without stopping, and since you don't know the area you had to be going to the station. You took the train to get here, right?"

He was right. Amon had been worried about getting caught in traffic, so he'd taken the train instead. *This guy looks rough but he notices more than I thought he would.*

"What made you want to be a detective?"

I don't really trust him much, but he must have a motivation to do this kind of work. Amon expected a positive answer, but instead, Morimine said, "It just happened."

"It just happened?"

"Yeah. I didn't really have any other options."

"But you must take some kind of pride in your work?"

"Pride?" Morimine scoffed, as if this were somehow contemptuous. "I don't have to take pride. Anyway, we're going to the station, yeah? I'll lead and you can catch up on your reading there. If there's something you don't get, just ask."

This guy goes storming into the CCG's offices, guns blazing, to get an investigation restarted and he has no pride in his work? Doesn't say much for his profession. Amon dropped the subject but continued thinking over his suspicions as he watched Morimine walk on ahead of him. His eyes fell to the notes Yanagi had given him. Three months ago, Mai Hirano was on her way home from an after-school

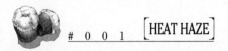

club meeting when she disappeared. She was not involved in illicit activities, and she was on good terms with all her friends.

There wasn't much in the way of witness statements. People who had seen high school–age girls that looked like her hadn't reported anything suspicious.

Searches turned up little in the way of concrete evidence, but eventually Mai's barrette was found.

However, the place where her barrette was found was... "Near the 8th Ward police station?"

"That's right. It was left in a prominent place just across from the station."

Then there was the deposit of bodily fluid from a Ghoul.

"Did someone find the barrette and bring it to that location?"

"If they did find it, why not just hand it in? Although maybe under the circumstances they couldn't."

"Under the circumstances..."

"Perhaps they were involved in the case."

Morimine turned to look at Amon.

"Look, Amon. Like I told you, I'm pretty sure this was the work of a human."

True, that's what he claimed when he was talking to Yanagi.

"What about this Ghoul fluid then?"

You know, the entire reason the CCG has to deal with this.

"Yeah... but the barrette was placed near the police station, right? Whoever put it there was counting on the police to find it, so whoever they wanted us to catch is probably human, in that case."

"Isn't that a bit too simplistic? The public has a friendlier relationship with the police than with the CCG. So there's nothing special about someone taking it directly to the police."

"You're way off, man." Morimine's tone had an implication to it. He turned his eyes away. "This story goes a lot deeper than that."

What does he mean by that?

"We're almost at the station," Morimine said, then clamped his mouth shut.

They spent that day walking around the area without making any real breakthroughs. When Amon said that he was going to leave it for the day and head back to the CCG, Morimine gave him a salute and said, "Thanks for your hard work," then walked off. He stopped and turned back to add, "See you tomorrow."

When he got back to the 8th Ward office, Yanagi and Tojo were waiting for him, their faces betraying their worry.

"You look beat, Amon. How'd it go?"

"Did things go all right with Morimine?"

"I've got absolutely no results to show for today."

"Well, results don't come that easily. The most important thing right now is for you to get acquainted with the area. Wanna come for a drink with us, Amon?" Yanagi mimicked waving a bottle. This, of course, also had implications of welcoming Amon to the ward and giving him information. In the old days, when he was full of passion

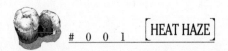

0 0 1 [HEAT HAZE]

for investigating Ghouls, he would not have looked favorably upon such an invitation, but now Amon replied, "Of course." This was how much of an influence Nakajima—the clerk investigator from the 20th Ward who followed Amon devotedly—and Shinohara had had on him, not just as an investigator but as a man.

The place Yanagi took him to was a little restaurant with a relaxed atmosphere.

"Why do you come to cheapo places like this when your wife's a great cook, Yanagi?"

"Tojo, shut it." Yanagi gave a little shove to Tojo, who grinned, as they headed into the dining room.

"You've got children, don't you, Yanagi?" Amon asked.

"I have a son. He's in elementary school. All of a sudden he says he wants to be a chef, because he wants everyone to be able to eat good food. Just like my wife," said Yanagi.

"A chef? It's great that he's got his sights set on something," Amon said in admiration as he sat down at the table. *Unlike Morimine, who just wound up in his job.*

"Well, he's still little so who knows . . . I mean, who knows if I'll still be alive when he's grown," Yanagi said nonchalantly. *As investigators, we come face to face with death. You never knew when it might be your turn. Investigators with families must spend a lot of time thinking about it.*

For a moment, the air was charged. Tojo noticed and responded sensitively.

"Yanagi, it's a little early to take the conversation somewhere that dark! You're gonna be fine, and you'll get to pig out on your grown son's cooking!"

But Yanagi reacted badly instead. "You're too damn positive, you know. You finally get this long-range ukaku Quinque that you've wanted for so long, and now you can't hit a target to save your life. You need to practice! Practice!"

"I am practicing! Am I not supposed to listen to what Noyama said?" Tojo embraced the attaché case next to him. *So, his Quinque is named Noyama*, Amon thought.

"You're really never gonna get promoted if you act like that," Yanagi said, his face showing his astonishment.

"You have an ukaku Quinque, Tojo?" Amon asked.

"That's right. Yanagi uses a bikaku on the front lines, so as backup..."

"Yeah, and because of you, I've almost been killed. If I don't live to see my son as a grown man, it'll be your fault, not a Ghoul's."

Ignoring Yanagi's grumbling, Tojo looked down at Amon's attaché case. "You use a kokaku, right Amon?"

"Yeah, it's called Kura."

"Kura?" Yanagi whispered, looking serious. "That was Mado's..." Indeed, Amon had inherited this Quinque from Mado, who was now deceased. And thanks to it, he had been able to defeat the bikaku of the Bin Brothers, two of the Ghouls who had executed the Aogiri attack.

"Did you know Mado, Yanagi?"

"Not well, but I've heard a lot about his Quinque. There are a lot

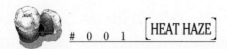

[HEAT HAZE]

of guys who talk about Mado, and I'm so bad at handling a Quinque that I'll be damned if I talk about anyone else, but I always envied Mado for his skill and knowledge when it came to handling one."

A memory of Mado clutching his precious attaché case arose in Amon's mind. Seeing the look on Amon's face, Yanagi cut in as if he'd suddenly remembered something.

"Speaking of Mado, how is his daught—?"

Before he could finish his thought, the waitress appeared with their food. "Sorry to have kept you waiting."

"Well, let's leave the talk about the old days there, shall we? Eat up, Amon. The food's really good here."

Amon would have liked to talk more about Mado, but he nodded and started eating.

"The thing is, though, if the culprit really is a Ghoul, then where did this Ghoul take that schoolgirl? I know they found her barrette with Ghoul fluids on it, but her body was never found. So I wonder if, instead, she actually ran away from home or something . . ."

"Tojo, if Morimine heard you say that he'd flip out."

"But then that means she might still be alive. Amon, what do you think?"

Amon set his chopsticks down.

"I have to be honest and say that at the present stage, I can't rule anything out. But . . ."

"But?"

Amon sat up stiffly. "If a Ghoul was involved we will find and destroy it. Absolutely."

"O-of course," Tojo nodded, taken aback by Amon's enthusiasm.

"For now, Amon, just keep your focus on the case."

"Yes sir."

———————

They stayed out drinking for three hours. Tojo started joking about moving on to somewhere else, but Yanagi cut him off.

Amon wanted to get a feel for the streets at night, so he said goodbye and walked alone through the 8th Ward.

No eyewitness testimony. No body. So it's possible that she was snatched off the street and taken somewhere private . . . Which means it's highly likely to be a Ghoul with an ukaku, Amon thought to himself.

Ghouls had physical abilities far superior to humans. And the instantaneous force of an ukaku would easily overwhelm someone.

Amon checked the case files that Yanagi had given him to see whether there were any Ghouls with ukaku in the 8th Ward who repeatedly preyed on humans.

But there weren't.

So it must be a Ghoul who recently arrived in the area. I should send a request to other branches asking if they have any information on a Ghoul with an ukaku known to prey on teenage girls, he thought, then checked his watch.

"I'll do it when I get home."

Amon picked up the attaché case containing his Quinque and

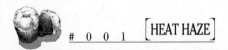

[HEAT HAZE]

headed to the train station.

This way's the shortcut, he thought, going down the side street that Morimine had showed him. The alley was small and narrow, with no lights to show the way. *Probably only locals know this route.*

He heard only the sound of his own footsteps echoing as he walked. Then, suddenly, he heard voices somewhere. They were getting louder as he kept walking.

As he proceeded he saw a young man and woman arguing at the end of the alley.

"What are you saying?! I want it all, as soon as possible!"

"I'm sorry, please, this has to be the last . . ."

It seemed like the man blamed her for something. Sobbing, she took a white envelope from her bag and handed it to the man. He snatched the envelope from her hands and checked the contents. To the naked eye, it looked like a huge wad of cash. *Is this blackmail?*

"Hey, what are you doing there?" Amon yelled, rushing up to the two of them. They both turned to look at him, and their eyes widened in surprise. As Amon started trying to subdue the man, the woman yelled, "No!" and spread her arms, trying to protect him.

"Do whatever you like, you stupid bitch!" The man ran off, clutching the envelope.

"Hey, wait!"

Amon tried to chase after him, but the woman grabbed him. "You don't understand, you don't understand," she said.

"Wasn't he just shaking you down?"

"Ah . . ."

Then they both gave a yelp of surprise.

As they stood there in the dimly lit side street, Amon finally got a good look at her face and saw that she was the sophisticated woman who had told him where to go that morning. *What's she doing out at night giving a wad of cash to that guy? What on earth is going on here?*

"I'm embarrassed that you saw that. I'm really sorry . . ."

She lowered her head in apology.

"But everything's fine."

She gave a weak smile and bowed again, then turned her back on Amon and started walking away. But her gait was unsteady.

Sure enough, she made it only three steps before she stumbled and hit the ground.

"Are you all right?" he called out.

"I'm sorry, I'm sorry . . ."

Amon lent her a hand to help her up, and she bowed her head apologetically again.

"Are you sure you can walk? How are you getting home?"

"Someone is waiting for me at the train station. So I'll be fine," she said.

She looks refined, and she may well be, but there's something suspicious about her. And what was that business with the money?

"I'm on my way to the station right now. Let's walk together."

Suddenly she looked at him suspiciously. "But . . ."

"This morning you helped me find the way to work. I owe you," he said.

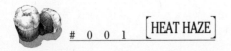

0 0 1 [HEAT HAZE]

It wasn't the only reason he wanted to accompany her, but something about what he said made her smile.

"Well . . . if you insist."

"I do."

They did not speak as they walked; the only sound was their footsteps. She walked slowly, taking ten minutes to walk what should've taken three or four.

As light from the main street began to filter into the alleyway, someone saw them and shouted, "Miss Koharu!" *Koharu. I suppose that's her name.* Amon saw the elderly woman who had been with her that morning rushing toward them. *Probably not her mother if she calls her "Miss."*

"Mrs. Otokaze, I'm sorry for making you wait . . ."

"It's fine, dear. And who is this?"

The elderly woman she called Mrs. Otokaze stared up at Amon presumptuously.

"I got lightheaded and he was worried about me, so he walked with me. I'm not sure if you remember, but we met him this morning," Koharu explained neatly, but Otokaze's eyes still searched Amon's face. She seemed wary of him. *Between the cryptic conversation earlier, the envelope stuffed full of cash, and Otokaze's attitude toward me, there's no doubt that Koharu is caught up in some kind of trouble.*

"I don't know what happened, but if there's something criminal going on, you should tell the police," Amon warned Koharu. "This is not the kind of thing you can just put up with until it goes away. Because other people could get hurt, not just you."

She might understand better if I talk about the impact on the people around her, rather than what might happen to herself. Amon's words seemed to make her look at herself in surprise.

"Other people. . . Oh, you're right, you really are. . ."

She nodded slightly as she mulled over what he'd said.

"You're too kind," she said and gave him a gentle smile. A blush spread across her pale cheek.

But Amon said flatly, "I'm not."

"Um, may I have your name?"

"My name? I'm Kotaro Amon."

"Kotaro. . . what a nice name. If there's anything I can do to show my gratitude. . ."

"Please, don't worry. I owe you for this morning."

"You really are too kind," she said. "Thank you." Koharu bowed deeply before disappearing with Otokaze into a taxi waiting at the station.

This place is wearing me out already and I just got here, Amon thought to himself. *First Detective Morimine, and now Koharu.*

Amon sighed and finally started on his way home.

0 0 1　[HEAT HAZE]

IV

It had been one week since he'd been sent to the 8th Ward, and Amon had spent all of his time searching for clues in the case of the missing schoolgirl. He was busy comparing alibis and checking where suspected Ghouls had been at the time of her disappearance. And next to him all the while was Lieutenant Morimine. He had followed Amon around every single day that week.

"There are two suspected Ghouls without alibis for the day of the girl's disappearance. I think we need to take a closer look at these two . . ."

"Well, I think they're all clear, myself," Morimine said with a sneer. "Just hurry up and get it signed off as not involving a Ghoul, and pass the case back to me."

And every day, Morimine undermined Amon's investigation in some way.

"Can you stop interfering with my investigation? And how can you even say that, when a Ghoul left fluids on her barrette? Obviously a Ghoul was somehow involved."

"A Ghoul might've been involved, but there's no way it was one of these suspected Ghouls."

"And what is your evidence?"

"That the barrette was left near the police station, not the CCG office."

Amon shook his head and put his hand to his face. *All he does is meddle in my investigation, and when I ask him for evidence to support his theory, that's all he has. And he has no other explanation.*

"If you're going to interfere with my investigation, just go back to the station. I'm sure you have other work to do."

"Sorry, man, but I'm staying here until you conclude your investigation."

Maybe he thinks that if he keeps putting pressure on me I'll get so frustrated I'll just quit. "Until we have evidence clearly showing that it wasn't a Ghoul, I'm not going to turn this case back over to you guys," Amon said, hammering the point home.

"Stubborn bastard," Morimine complained bluntly.

"And what's so wrong with being stubborn? I don't want to compromise the investigation."

"God, you're so green it hurts . . ."

"Are you mocking me?"

"Not at all. But you spend so much time looking straight ahead that you can't see what's around you."

Amon started to head back to the office. Morimine followed him, looking fed up.

I've had people tell me I'm stubborn before, but Morimine really is pigheaded.

I'm going to investigate this myself. If I let him get to me there'll be no end to it. The fact that he's throwing me off at all annoys me. What's most important now is to check out these two people who don't have alibis, Amon thought as he walked, surveying his surroundings.

Just then a woman he knew he'd seen before came into sight.

"Huh?"

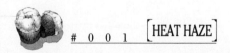

0 0 1 [HEAT HAZE]

"Someone you know?" asked the ever-observant Morimine.

"Oh, no . . ."

What a small world. On the other side of the road, walking with her face slightly down, was Koharu following after Otokaze.

"Wait—I know that woman too."

So even Morimine knows her. "An acquaintance of yours?" Amon asked.

He shook his head. "Not an acquaintance. I took a statement from her once. She's beautiful, she's always with someone, and I remember that when I showed her my badge, she was strangely surprised," he said.

"By your badge?"

"Yeah. I mean, it's just a badge, nothing unusual about it."

Amon had to agree; when Morimine had showed it to him there hadn't been anything particularly odd about it.

"She seemed somehow tragic."

"Tragic how?"

"Well, look, a woman with a pretty face all dolled up like that? She should have so much confidence in herself that she practically floats down the street. But the way she's walking, it's like she wants to avoid anyone looking at her. There's an air of anxiety around her."

Amon watched her walk and thought that Morimine was being a little over-the-top, but he also remembered how she had looked a week ago as she handed over the money to that man.

"Morimine, have there been any reports from victims of blackmail or anything like that to the police this week?"

"Don't know what that's got to do with what we're talking about, but no, I haven't heard anything. Wait, you think she's being blackmailed?"

"No, I don't know for sure."

Amon told him about what he'd seen on his first day. "Hmm," Morimine murmured, watching her walk into the hospital down the street.

———————————

Amon went back to the branch office with barely anything to show for his time. Yanagi and Tojo were out meeting with investigators from the 7th Ward, where the Ghoul restaurant was located. Amon checked their report for the day and then left the office.

He knew the way to the train station very well now. In his head he went over his plans for the next day as he turned down the alleyway. *You know, I wonder how they're doing back in the 20th Ward.* Seido Takizawa, a rank 2 investigator who seemed to idolize Amon, had told him that if anything happened they'd call him. *And they haven't, so I guess nothing's happened. But it also means there's been no progress.*

"And they haven't gotten the Rabbit yet . . ."

The Rabbit was Amon's responsibility—a small Ghoul with a light body who knew their way around an ukaku. The Rabbit had killed a young clerk investigator named Kusaba—whose round glasses had been his trademark—and Mado, a man Amon had

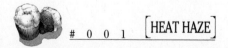

respected with all his heart. Amon felt he had to uncover the Rabbit's identity and avenge their deaths in tribute.

But there was another reason why Amon was pursuing the Rabbit. The Ghoul with the eye patch that he'd seen during the Aogiri battle was thought to have some connection to the Rabbit. There was something Amon wanted to ask him.

"I can't afford to stall."

If he didn't get to work on the task he'd given himself, there was no way he would find those two Ghouls. Amon turned back the way he had just came. *The case of the missing schoolgirl. Even if there's little evidence or information, I've gotta investigate more thoroughly to get answers.* Amon's stride was long as he walked.

"Ack!"

But soon he ran smack into something and heard a woman cry out. Apparently he had bumped into a woman near him. "Sorry, you okay?" he said, apologizing hastily, but when he saw her face his confusion returned. "You're . . ."

It was Koharu, who he'd seen just that afternoon. And this time the old woman who had called her "Miss" wasn't with her.

"Oh, I'm . . . I'm fine. I'm sorry, I didn't warn you in time."

The ground around her was littered with things she had been carrying. There were even some cupcakes lying there. Seeing this, Koharu rushed to pick them up.

"I knew you worked at the CCG, so I thought if I waited nearby I might run into you . . . I wanted to give you this to thank you. But . . ."

She looked at the crumpled box with the cupcakes in it, which she had apparently brought to give to Amon.

"You have nothing to thank me for."

"No, it made me very happy that someone I don't even know was so kind to me. But there's no way I can give you this now . . ." she muttered, looking at the smashed cupcakes.

Amon reached over smoothly and took one. He lightly brushed the dirt off the surface and tossed the cupcake into his mouth.

"Oh."

A bit gritty but it tastes good. Although not quite sweet enough for a sweet tooth like myself.

"Is it all right?" Koharu asked fearfully.

"Very good," he said, bringing his hands together in thanks.

"I'm glad. I know most men don't like sweet things, so I got ones that were a little less sweet . . ."

"Perhaps it could've been a little sweeter." Amon picked up his attaché case from the ground. "On another note, have you reported what happened the other night to the police?"

"I . . . I'm not really sure what to do."

"How so?"

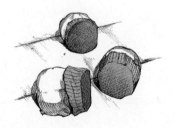

"I still haven't made my mind up about a lot of things." She didn't make it clear, but it seemed like she was considering her options.

"It's better for you to speak honestly," Amon said, giving her a few words of advice, and then left.

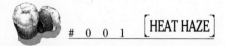

0 0 1   [HEAT HAZE]

V

"Amon, you gotta stop staying here overnight. You all right?" Yanagi called out, surprised to see Amon there already, sorting through documents on his own and collecting data.

"Morning. My body is disciplined so it's not much of a problem." Since the day he'd decided to really dedicate himself to the case, Amon had been staying in the office overnight trying to find clues in the case of the missing schoolgirl.

"You're nothing if not predictable, I gotta say. Give Tojo some of whatever you're drinking, man. Anyway, found anything?" Yanagi said, peeking over his shoulder. Amon showed him a flier.

"What's this? 'Have you seen this child? Please call'... Did you make this? No, it looks old, and the name's wrong. Who is Haruka Seta?"

Amon was meant to be investigating the disappearance of Mai Hirano. But this flier was regarding a girl named Haruka Seta. And the paper had turned reddish brown in the sun.

"Oh, the date of her disappearance is eighteen years ago."

"That's right, Yanagi. Eighteen years ago a similar incident happened in the 8th Ward."

The picture on the flier was of a very serious-looking girl. And she, too, had suddenly and uncharacteristically disappeared.

"That's not all. I found this in the newspaper—fifteen years ago another girl went missing in this Ward."

Amon showed him a photocopy of a newspaper.

"If there's no sign of Ghoul involvement, sometimes the CCG just doesn't hear about a case . . . I might turn up more of these if I keep looking."

"You're right, you know. Maybe this case goes a lot deeper than we thought . . ."

Amon had a sudden sense of déjà vu and could not get any words out. *I've heard those words before.* Finally the memory came to him—Morimine talking about the case.

"This story goes a lot deeper than that."

"You think Morimine knows?" Yanagi asked, as if he had read Amon's mind.

"If he does, he hasn't told me anything."

"Right . . . He seems like the kind of guy who would tell you if he knew. But I think it's kind of strange that he doesn't know. If you found this kind of information, then the police must have it too. Amon, I want you to check with Morimine. You think he'll be coming around today?"

Amon looked at the clock. It was almost time for him to arrive. Amon stood up, flier in hand. When he went out the CCG's front door and looked around he saw Morimine crouching amidst the lush greenery, smoking a cigarette. He noticed Amon immediately, stubbed out his cigarette and stood up.

"You're a bit early today."

Morimine shoved his hands in his pockets and ambled over. Amon held out the flier in his hand.

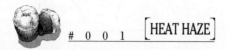

0 0 1 [HEAT HAZE]

"What's this?" He took it from Amon, holding it up so he could see. "Huh..." he grunted. "This thing takes me back."

"Eighteen years ago there was a similar case in this area. Did you know about this?"

Morimine glanced up at Amon. "As a cop, no, I did not know about this," he said.

"What do you mean, 'as a cop'?" *Is he speaking on behalf of the organization? All right, I'll change my question.*

"What about as an individual?"

I have here a guy who just keeps saying that because the barrette was left near the police station it must be the work of a human. But after that answer I wonder if there's some real reason, some information only he knows.

Morimine was silent, as if he was considering something. Just when Amon lost patience and was about to tear him apart, Morimine spoke.

"This girl... Haruka Seta, who went missing eighteen years ago, disappeared on her way home from watching some fireworks."

The flier didn't have that piece of information on it. Morimine continued in a neutral tone.

"Fifteen years ago, another girl suddenly disappeared. And thirteen years ago too, although that happened one ward over, in the 7th."

He didn't pause to recall, nor did he stutter as he went through his memories. It was like he'd beaten the information into his mind.

And that fact made Amon feel even angrier.

Morimine continued, his voice clear. "Then nine years ago a girl was kidnapped in the 23rd Ward on her way home from a voice training class, and seven years ago . . ."

Amon grabbed him by the lapels. "If you knew all of that, why did you keep quiet about it until now?" *If we'd had all of this information, it might've changed the investigation. But more than that, I'm furious with him for berating me all this time when he was withholding information about the case. For a guy who likes to remind you that a human life is at stake here, this is incredibly irresponsible.*

But Morimine's expression did not change in the slightest, as if he already knew how Amon had arrived at this answer and that he was being blamed.

"Listen, Amon. At the time that Haruka Seta, probably the first victim in this case, went missing, it was barely investigated and she was treated as a runaway."

Amon let go of Morimine's lapels and took another look at the flier.

"I looked into the disappearances in the other wards, too, and in some cases Ghoul involvement was suspected and the CCG cooperated in the investigation. But the investigations all ended without much in the way of results."

Morimine stopped there for a second and sighed.

"And the connection between them was ignored, and now, in this case in the 8th Ward, a barrette has been found with a Ghoul's bodily fluids on it. What drives me crazy is that there's one guy who decided eighteen years ago, when Haruka Seta disappeared, that

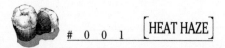

she'd run away and there was no need to investigate. And that guy is now at the top of the Criminal Division."

"You don't mean . . ."

"He doesn't want Haruka Seta's case to be dredged up and tied in with this case, all to protect his own damn neck. The police and all the newspapers hounded Haruka's mother, saying that there had been problems at home, and in the end, she couldn't take it and killed herself."

Is there some kind of corruption going on here?

Morimine gave a grim, self-mocking smile. "If the culprit is a Ghoul then they can be taken down without argument. And then the Haruka Seta case can sort of be put to rest. That's what the higher-ups are hoping. But with such a passionate Ghoul investigator on the case that doesn't seem possible. I mean, look at all this old stuff you've managed to dig up," he said, sounding impressed. But that was not what Amon was looking to hear.

"Morimine, you've told me time and time again that you believe this was the work of a human. Do you have some reason to think that?"

"Like I keep saying, the barrette was dropped near the police station. That's the biggest reason. Because, you know, since eighteen years ago the same kind of disappearances have kept happening, but not a single piece of evidence connected to the perpetrator had ever emerged. Maybe that's just because the culprit is very careful. But this time, this barrette appeared. It got me thinking."

Morimine, who always seemed very detached, now wore an

expression of anguish. It was the first time Amon had seen him look that way. "Someone put it there because they were counting on us, the police. They want us to catch the culprit. That's why I think the culprit is human."

There was something incomprehensible about Morimine's theory to Amon. But there was also something strangely sincere about the way he spoke. However, there were some points that Amon just couldn't concede.

"I can understand the police's position here. But I think a Ghoul was involved in this case in some form, for more reasons than just the fluids on the barrette."

Morimine said nothing.

"I can't just let that go, and I think we have to find that Ghoul before we can get any closer to the truth about what happened in this case. So again, I cannot simply turn this case back over to the police."

Scratching his head, Morimine grumbled, "God, you've got a stick up your ass." But he had a smile on his face. "Well then, I'm with you to the bitter end."

Morimine gave Amon information about all the similar incidents that had occurred over the last eighteen years. Then they looked at all the suspected Ghouls to see how they applied to the cases. Thanks to Morimine's cooperation and the avalanche of information

he supplied, the investigation had picked up momentum, but all the answers that emerged were rather lacking.

"None of them could've done it . . ."

After looking into the suspected Ghoul who lived near the police station, Amon stared at the documents given to him by Yanagi, muttering to himself. Everyone who had been considered suspicious had an alibi.

This investigation is just going nowhere. The CCG has done all it can, so maybe this is one of those times we could turn it back over to the police.

However, Morimine wasn't in as big a hurry as before.

"Did you get information from other wards about suspected Ghouls? And Ghouls that prey upon teenage girls?"

"I requested it, but inevitably, there are a lot of suspected Ghouls living outside of the 8th Ward."

"I guess it's more difficult for you to leave your post and go off searching, since you're temporarily in charge of the ward. And I guess you can't hand the contents over to me due to confidentiality . . ."

They were at a standstill in front of the station. Morimine shrugged. "Well, we can't just stand around here and talk about it all day. Let's go talk tactics somewhere," he said.

"Good idea . . . We can borrow the meeting room at the CCG for now."

"All right."

Amon took the lead and turned down the side street that led to the CCG's building. As soon as they started down the alley, which was sandwiched between two tall buildings, it was suddenly rather dark. But Amon was used to it now, since he often came this way.

After a short while, they could see a sliver light at the end of the alley. At the same time, they also saw a shadow coming toward them. Amon squinted into the sunlight trying to see who it was. It was Koharu.

"Oh, hello, Kotaro," she said, bowing her head deeply. Then Morimine, who had been walking behind Amon, entered her line of sight. She gasped in surprise, staring intently at his face.

"And you're . . . a detective."

"That's right."

Morimine had said before that he remembered her from taking her statement once, but she also seemed to remember him.

"I'm sorry, are you on duty right now?"

"We are. Has something happened?" Amon said.

"Um, well . . ." she stuttered, looking at Morimine. Feeling like he was interrupting something, Morimine looked at Amon and Koharu, then walked a short distance away. *Looked at from the outside this must seem like a scene from a romantic movie. Her response was certainly polite, and she appears, for all intents and purposes, to be a normal woman, faultless in every way.* Yet Amon turned a skeptical eye toward her.

"So, what is this about?"

Koharu took a paper bag out of her handbag.

"What is it?"

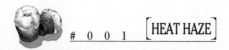 # 0 0 1 [HEAT HAZE]

"You said that you wished the cake I gave you before was sweeter so . . . here." She handed the bag over. Amon looked inside and saw a cupcake. It smelled much sweeter than the one she had given him before—much more to Amon's taste. But characteristically, a frown passed over Amon's face.

"I keep telling you, it's not a big deal. If you don't quit doing this it's going to put me in a difficult position."

"Y-yes, of course, you're right. But the one you ate was dirty, and I'm very sorry . . ." Koharu said, flustered. She blushed and looked down.

"What's wrong with you, Amon, man? You gotta say thank you when someone gives you something," said Morimine, lighting a cigarette. He was apparently still paying attention although he was facing the opposite direction.

"Interrupting me like this in the middle of the workday to discuss something private is not all right," Amon said.

"You really do have a stick up your ass, you know," Morimine said, exhaling a cloud of smoke. He turned to look Koharu, peeking from behind Amon.

"Forget that—lady, you look very pale. You look a little unwell— I thought that before when I saw you. Do you have some kind of illness or something?"

"Oh, no, I . . . my adoptive father collapsed and he's in the hospital. I've been caring for him. I guess it must show," Koharu said, putting her hands to her face.

"You're adopted?"

"Yes. I lost my parents when I was young . . ."

"How?"

She did not answer.

"In an accident or what?"

It was just like he was grilling her. Koharu's mouth twisted and she looked down slowly. Morimine stared at her, waiting for her to answer.

"Amon? Is that you?"

Just then another voice echoed down the alley. Three men, coming from the direction of the station, walked up to join them. It was Yanagi and Tojo, followed by . . .

"Hard at work, Amon?"

He had sharp eyes and slicked-back hair.

"Fura!"

It was Taishi Fura, the investigator in charge of the 7th Ward, where the Ghoul restaurant was located.

"What are you doing here?"

"I thought I'd come check on things in the 8th. I've been on patrol with Yanagi . . ." Fura trailed off, finally taking notice of Morimine and Koharu's presence.

"Oh, this is Lieutenant Morimine, who is assisting me with an investigation right now, and this is . . . a resident of the area."

Amon had no problem introducing Morimine, but he hesitated for a moment over how to describe Koharu. He hated having conversations unrelated to work while he was on duty, not only because it stalled his investigation, but also because things like this happened.

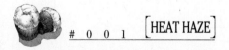

0 0 1 [HEAT HAZE]

"I see. We're heading back to the branch office now, but it looks like you might've been on your way back too. See you later."

"Yes sir."

Fura, Yanagi, and Tojo passed them and went off.

"So you really do work for the CCG," Koharu said, once they'd faded into the distance.

"Yes. I am a Ghoul investigator."

"Oh . . . I hear that's a very dangerous job. I've been hearing a lot about some disturbing Ghoul incidents lately too. Doesn't it scare you?"

Amon often got these kinds of questions from civilians. His answer was always the same: "Of course, I'm terrified by Ghouls, and I've lost a lot of colleagues to them over the years. But still, somebody has to do it."

She looked at him.

"I cannot stand by and watch innocent people be attacked and killed by Ghouls. And what's more, I don't want to see more people in the world who have lost someone important to them. That's why I'm out here eradicating Ghouls and trying to return some order to the world. That is the mission that has been given to us at the CCG."

As Koharu listened, her eyes grew very serious. "That's incredible," she exclaimed with a sigh. Then, she started to speak as if she'd made her mind up. "Kotaro, the truth is . . . my parents were caught up in an incident and killed."

"What did you say?" This unexpected confession made Amon look at her in surprise.

"It was a dark night, and the moon was hidden behind the clouds . . . We were all just about to go to bed when a group of men I didn't know came. My father and mother were . . . both killed."

So that's why she clammed up when Morimine asked her.

"The man who took care of me after I lost my parents is my adoptive father. But now he's confined to bed and he hasn't got much time left. So I do understand how it feels to lose people who are important to you."

As he listened to her story, Amon was also remembering things. The things that happened in the orphanage, where he'd lived with other children who had lost their parents. But the memories were blurry in his mind, as if seen through a heat haze.

"When I heard what you had to say, I realized that I have to find my own way in the world. Sorry for keeping you from your work again and again. Thank you," Koharu said, and smiled.

After Koharu left, Morimine, who had been watching the entire time, turned to Amon and said, "So you're a man of the flesh, too."

"A man of the flesh?" Amon echoed.

"Yeah, that's why you've got such a stick up your ass. Did a woman hurt you or something?"

"What are you talking about?" Amon asked Morimine, who looked amazed.

"If I explained you probably wouldn't get it," he said lightly.

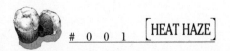 # 0 0 1 [HEAT HAZE]

Unsatisfied with this answer, Amon wanted to question him in detail, but Morimine gave him a pat on the shoulder. "Right, I gotta get back to the CCG. I got stuff to do. I'll leave you here."

But I thought we were going to plan out a strategy, Amon thought, confused, as Morimine dashed off.

"What was that about?"

———————

"Hey, Amon, that girl you were with is beautiful!" Tojo said tactlessly when Amon got back to the CCG office. *I suppose he's talking about Koharu. She does seem to have something appealing to most men.*

"It was the first time we'd met, but she was looking right at me with those big, round eyes. I found it unnerving."

"You're too self-conscious, man, if you get scared because a girl stares at you," Yanagi said, jumping into the conversation. His face looked sour. But Tojo didn't seem to hear him.

Then, Fura, who had come to the 8th Ward to take a look at some documents, cut in. "You don't know anything about her," he said.

What do you mean?"

"There's always another side to people, even people that look that good on the outside. So don't put your own expectations on someone you don't know that well."

"Ha, look, Tojo—what you said is so stupid it disgusted Fura too!"

Yanagi hit Tojo on the head like a parent scolding a child.

"No, I just said that because of some experiences I had when I was a younger man," Fura added, followed by a wry smile.

Amon agreed with Fura, too. *Even Ghouls can put on a good face in front of people and then eat someone without batting an eyelid.*

"Ghouls," Amon muttered quietly, then opened the paper bag he was carrying and took out the cupcake. He brought it up to his nose and took a sniff, but there was nothing particularly strange about the smell. He took a bite just to check.

Is there really nothing strange about it?

The flavor was much sweeter and better than the one he'd eaten before. But something about the way Koharu acted and spoke made him feel uneasy.

Amon hid his thoughts from his face as he returned the cupcake, with one bite taken out of it, to the paper bag.

After the meeting ended and he'd said goodbye to Fura, Yanagi, and Tojo, Amon was once again left on his own in the 8th Ward branch office. It was almost midnight. Deciding to take a little break to go buy a hot drink, Amon stood up from his desk.

Suddenly, his cell phone started ringing. It was Morimine. *He's never called me this late before*, Amon puzzled as he answered. "Hello, this is Amon."

"Amon, are you still at the CCG office?" Morimine was almost shouting.

"Yeah, I'm here . . ."

"I'm at the door. Sorry, but could you let me in?"

He sounded somehow in a rush. Amon kept his phone to his ear as he hurried out of the room.

"Has something happened?"

"It's about Koharu Utsumi, that tragic-looking girl."

"Utsumi . . . ?"

He'd known her name but not her family name. *I don't know why he brought up her name, but I have a bad feeling about this.*

"Can you go around the back? I'll be right there," Amon said, ending the call as he rushed into the elevator. It took what felt like an incredibly long time to reach the ground floor. When he finally got to the back entrance and opened the door, Morimine was standing there with a grim expression on his face.

"What's happened?"

"I ran some checks on her today. I went to the hospital she said her adoptive father was in and I checked his name."

"Why did you do that?"

"Call it detective's intuition," Morimine said, holding his hand to his forehead. "You don't believe me?"

Maybe Morimine doesn't think that a solid guy like me could be swayed by something that sounds as uncertain as the word "intuition." But the words hit him like a rock.

"Tell me everything."

Now Morimine was the one being interrogated as Amon led him into his office, sitting across the desk from him.

"Her adoptive father's name is Yujiro Utsumi. He's the president of a trading company that's well-known around here. And his adopted daughter, Koharu, is twenty-eight years old. When I asked people in the neighborhood, they said she seemed to have been adopted eighteen years ago."

Eighteen years ago. That number sent chills down Amon's spine. *The same year that Haruka Seta went missing.*

"So I looked into it. To see if there was a case eighteen years ago where a couple was killed and only their child survived."

If they were murdered the police should still have the case files.

But Morimine said, "I didn't look very thoroughly, so maybe something got past me but . . . there wasn't anything."

"Nothing?"

"We've never had that kind of case."

Then she's lying. Seeing the doubt on Amon's face, Morimine

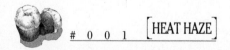

said, "But I think she was telling the truth."

"Then why is there no case?"

"Amon . . ." Morimine said, looking straight into his eyes. Another possibility began to arise in Amon's mind.

"Does the CCG have any information?"

That would mean . . .

"Did an investigator sneak into their home on a moonless night to exterminate a family of Ghouls?"

Amon could see the scene in his mind. He imagined an investigator pressed to the wall, listening in at night, when the whole family would have been together.

"And now that I think about it, it was just after I took her statement that time that Mai's barrette was left near the police station. And she seemed a little uncomfortable in places as she told that story today. She could've just said 'father' instead of 'adoptive father,' and if she overheard what happened it must stick in her mind, but then she just started confessing about her childhood . . ."

Then Amon's phone rang again. He wanted to hear more, but when he looked to see who was calling he was shocked.

"It's Yanagi."

Yanagi wasn't the kind of person to call this late without a very good reason.

Morimine also seemed to grasp that clearly. "You'd better pick up," he said, and Amon answered the phone.

"Amon, sorry for calling so late. But there's something I want to ask you about."

Yanagi sighed deeply. "When Tojo and I left the office tonight we were on our way to a bar when we ran into the woman that you were talking about. She seemed to recognize us too, and spoke to us. Then Tojo got all cocky and exchanged numbers with her . . ."

"He did what?!"

From Amon's words and behavior, Morimine guessed that something was up. His face turned gloomy.

"Yeah. Then, while we were drinking, he got a message from her asking if he wanted to go for dinner. I told him not to trust a woman who invites him to dinner just after meeting him, and he seemed to agree, but . . ."

"Tell me he didn't."

"When we got done drinking, he started joking about having another round like always, but then he left quickly. Later I got kind of concerned and sent him a message but he never replied. And when I try to call him, the call doesn't go through."

Bad feeling. Sixth sense. I haven't determined that she's a Ghoul. But something is urging me on.

"Morimine, do you know her address?"

"Yeah. I found it."

All the experience Amon had gained as an investigator told him that danger was at hand. Morimine nodded firmly, and Amon did in return.

"Yanagi, I think Tojo is in danger!"

"Danger? What kind of danger?"

"We have to find him immediately!"

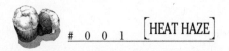 # 0 0 1 [HEAT HAZE]

He hung up and started running, attaché case in hand.

"Amon, my car's parked outside, let's take that!"

It was the time of night when most people were already asleep. Morimine stomped on the accelerator and headed to Koharu's house. As they drove Amon got in touch with Yanagi and explained the full circumstances.

"We're here!"

Her house, near the river, was a mansion with details that seemed more appropriate somewhere far from the 8th Ward. When they got out of the car, Amon could smell the sea. *I guess the tide has come up into the river.*

Amon clenched his attaché case in his hand and walked to the gate. He rang the doorbell but there was no response. They peeked through a gap in the sturdy gate, which was much taller than they were, and saw that lights were on in the back of the house. Then they heard some music playing quietly.

"What should we do?" Morimine asked.

This is an urgent matter. If it's all a misunderstanding then I'll take the punishment gladly.

"Morimine, get down."

Amon flung the hand holding his attaché case out and shook it hard to get through to the Quinque's biometric authentication system.

"Whoa!"

The attaché case, which looked just like an everyday model, opened with great force, and what was stuffed inside made a sound as it took its form.

"Holy shi—"

Amon's weapon of justice had appeared in the blink of an eye. It had shown its full power as Amon's companion in the Aogiri incident, but this Quinque, Kura, had originally belonged to Mado, Amon's respected superior. Its shape mimicked that of a giant sword, and even among other kokaku it was the heaviest of the heavyweight. Its weight served to maximize Amon's power.

Amon gave Kura a big swing, then turned his attention from warming up to the gate.

"We'll figure out a reason later!"

But you can't take back a human life. Amon pulled Kura back, then took a big step forward and struck the gate like he was trying to break through it with a ram.

"Agh!"

The sound of the impact was a heavy thud. The sturdy gate bent like a piece of wire in the face of the Quinque's attack and was blown away.

"Morimine, if it turns out she is a Ghoul, then we're in danger too. Once we're in there we'll have no margin for error, so if push comes to shove you might have to save me!"

Amon headed straight to the house. Morimine followed after him. "You're not human, you know," he said, teasingly.

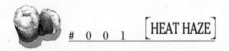 # 0 0 1 [HEAT HAZE]

He looked back at Morimine and said plainly, "No, I'm an investigator!"

————————————————

Once he'd broken through the locked door, a high-ceilinged reception hall appeared before them. As one would expect from a trader's house, the room was decorated with lots of art pieces and luxurious chandeliers. Classical music was playing loudly from an antique record player.

"I didn't think you'd come this quickly."

Further down the hallway a door leading to another room swung open and a woman quietly emerged. *That pale skin, those tragic eyes . . . That's Koharu, all right.*

"Is that . . . ?"

In her right hand, Koharu held a showy attaché case with a disproportionate amount of silver on it. Amon was familiar with the item—it was Tojo's Quinque.

"What have you done with Tojo, you bitch?"

Koharu said nothing. Instead she moved aside a screen that had been placed in a corner of the room. Behind it was a large table draped in a luxurious embroidered cloth, hiding something. She pulled the cloth away slowly.

"Tojo!"

"Mmf, mmf!"

His hands and feet were bound and he was gagged. She moved

away from him quickly, and Amon and Morimine rushed over to Tojo, staying wary of Koharu.

"What have you gotten yourself into, Tojo!"

"Ah! S-sorry. You found me!"

Morimine removed the gag and started undoing the ropes that bound his arms together. Amon turned around to face Koharu, shielding the other two. She held Tojo's attaché case to her chest.

"What on earth did you do this for?"

This woman had made Amon cupcakes to say thank you and praised his work as an investigator. *That was all just a front*, he thought, and suddenly felt sick. Koharu had no answer to Amon's question. She looked down, shutting her eyes tightly.

Something dense and foglike began to rise from Koharu's shoulders. Amon, the first to realize what it was, closed the distance between them at once, swinging his Quinque down. Koharu leapt back as far as she could, and as she pulled off a magnificent landing, her eyes opened.

"Her eyes are . . . red . . ."

Her kakugan.

"She's a Ghoul!"

The incessant overflow of Rc cells had created a set of thin wings on Koharu's back, just like dragonfly wings. She leapt backward again to create some more distance. Amon followed her.

The body of an Ukaku Ghoul was top class, but their attacks were lighter and no match for the kokaku, which provides serious defense. Wielding a kokaku Quinque, Amon had the advantage. He

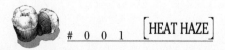

0 0 1 [HEAT HAZE]

kicked over a sculpture that was about six feet tall, blocking the direction that Koharu was headed, and then he swung Kura with all the force in his body.

She stuck out the attaché case she was holding and blocked Kura's swing with it. A crack formed in Tojo's case, but because it was made especially to contain Quinque, it was not totally destroyed. Koharu had nothing to counter the vibration that came at her through the attaché case. It flew backward, cushioning her impact.

"N-no! Not my Quinque!"

Amon could hear Tojo's pitiful screams, but for now his top priority was to destroy Koharu. Not letting up, he swung Kura again.

"Damn!"

But Koharu was skilled with the use of Tojo's attaché case, and she dodged Amon's attacks. *Did she steal Tojo's attaché case just for this?*

Naturally, when a Ghoul was faced with an investigator, they would attack in order to protect themselves. This increased the possibility for injury, but after they attacked there would inevitably be an opening. An investigator would use this to repel and destroy them—or that's how it always had been, but Koharu showed no sign of attacking. She did not try to cover the distance between them, instead devoting herself instead to defense. If she played it like that, her ukaku boasted a quickness that would make her difficult to catch. *Is she trying to wear me out, and then come at me?*

Amon rejected that thought. Ukaku required a dramatically higher consumption of Rc cells compared to other types of Kagune, and so was ill-suited to a long battle. *If she knows anything about her own Kagune then there's no way she'd have this kind of circuitous fighting style. But I can't figure out what her intention is.*

Don't think, he castigated himself.

The only thing I need to do as an investigator is destroy this Ghoul. If I keep attacking without pause and make her keep using her Kagune, eventually she'll run out of steam. This is what I trained for.

"Hahhhh!"

Amon put all of his force on the middle of Kura's long blade. The blade split into two. Kura was a transformable weapon. By dividing Kura down the middle to create a new blade, he now had two weapons. While Koharu's eyes were still wide in surprise at the Quinque's transformation, Amon threw one of the blades at her like a boomerang.

She yelped in shock.

Koharu tried to defend herself from the unexpected attack with the attaché case, but she could not protect herself against a flying, violently rotating Quinque.

"Ah!"

The attaché case flew away from her and, unable to withstand the momentum, she fell to the floor. Amon grasped Kura to himself, wanting to land the finishing blow. But Koharu was releasing large quantities of Rc cells, and even as she forced herself to stand up she avoided Amon's attack. Then she picked up the Quinque that Amon had thrown and jumped atop the chandelier.

Dammit!

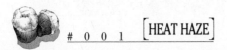 # 0 0 1 [HEAT HAZE]

The chandelier swung left and right under her weight. Koharu leaned against the chain connecting the chandelier to the ceiling, pushing and pulling violently with her shoulders. Her winglike Kagune gathered around her shoulders like a dense fog. She seemed to have lost her momentum when she released all of those Rc cells at once after avoiding Amon's attack.

Now was Amon's chance, but she'd escaped to a place he couldn't reach. He was wondering whether he should throw the Kura he still held in his right hand.

"Wait, Amon!"

Morimine's voice echoed in his ears. When he looked over, he saw that the lieutenant had a gun pointed at Koharu.

"Morimine! If you're not using Q Bullets, the ones specially developed for use against Ghouls, there's no point!"

"I'm going for it!"

He narrowed one eye, then took aim and fired.

"Gah!"

The bullet hit the chain Koharu was leaning against. She instinctively removed her hand from the shaking chain, which broke her balance, and she started to fall along with the chandelier.

"Nice one!"

Amon got his Quinque ready again.

"Whoa!"

"Wha—!"

But before Amon could attack, a hail of bullets much more powerful than those from Morimine's gun hit her. Her body was pierced

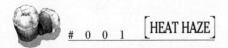

through countless times.

Amon and Morimine's eyes grew wide in surprise, but Tojo was even more surprised.

"I was just operating it, I didn't mean to—"

Apparently while he'd been checking the condition of his Quinque, the Quinque had attacked without Tojo intending it to do so, and it had shot Koharu with ukaku Quinque bullets. *Maybe his Quinque, used in place of a shield and now cracked, just malfunctioned.*

But the result was that they were able to capture Koharu. Her bloody body was thrown to the ground, and Koharu's breathing was heavy.

"Ko . . . taro . . ." Even in such circumstances, her eyes wet with blood, Koharu called out his name. "I'm . . . sorry . . ."

He'd just realized she was saying something when she apologized. Her eyes turned to Morimine, who walked over to look.

"You . . . too . . . Kyo . . . hei . . ."

"Huh? How's she know my name?" Morimine said in confusion. Kyohei was his name, but almost nobody ever called him that.

Koharu did not answer. She looked up at Amon and Morimine, choking out a few words.

"I . . . took them all. And then . . . I ate them . . ."

"What?!"

"They're . . . all . . . in that room," she said, pointing weakly at the other room further down the hall.

Her eyes started filling up with something that wasn't blood.

"I lived . . . from crime . . . to crime . . . But . . ."

Her eyes focused on Amon.

"Watching . . . you, Kotaro . . . gave me . . . courage . . ." She blinked, and tears spilled from her eyes. "I hope the future . . . that you want . . . comes to pass."

With her Kagune out of sight and her eyes closed, she looked just like a human. "That somehow . . . this world that we were born into can be . . ."

She was a Ghoul, but her last wish was that a Ghoul investigator's hope for the future would come true. It sounded like a prayer from the bottom of her heart.

And then she breathed her last.

"What does that mean?" Amon stood stunned over her, unable to understand her last words.

"Just what it sounds like," Morimine murmured. He stood next to Amon, looking down at Koharu with pity.

"Anything born doesn't want to die—no matter what they are. She was born a Ghoul and she had to live as a Ghoul. And that means eating people . . ."

So it was her wish that Ghouls themselves would disappear from this world?

"You gonna take a look in that room? We might find some answers in there, you know."

The room where she'd said they all were. Amon and Morimine walked in slowly.

"This is . . ."

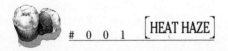

0 0 1 [HEAT HAZE]

In a complete reversal from the luxurious hall, this room seemed to have been used as a storage room. The walls had two tiers of shelves along them, on which sat neat boxes about ten inches to a side.

"Hey, look at . . ."

When Morimine took the box closest to them down from the shelf, he could see that the box was labeled MAI HIRANO. Immediately he shouted, "That's the missing girl's name!"

Mai Hirano, the owner of the barrette that was dropped off near the police station.

Morimine set the box down on the floor and, looking apprehensive, he opened the lid. Inside, the box was filled with personal belongings: a school uniform, a bag, and other things.

"These are the clothes Mai was supposed to be wearing when she went missing . . ."

But that wasn't all.

"There's . . . bones. And hair . . ."

Is that her? The bones and hair were in a plastic bag. Morimine started checking each of the other boxes on the shelves.

"And this one . . . And this one, too. They're all names of girls who went missing."

Then, suddenly, as if he'd realized something, he started running to the farthest shelves. He pulled the boxes down roughly, looked at the names on them and stopped moving.

"Morimine?"

The way he was behaving was completely different than

anything Amon had seen from him before. His hands were shaking as he opened the box and looked inside. Seeing the bones, hair, school uniform, and notebook inside, his face twisted up.

He screamed, "Haruka!"

Haruka. That name also sounded familiar to Amon. No, it *was* familiar. The letters of her name, the girl who had disappeared eighteen years ago, appeared in his mind: Haruka Seta.

"Morimine..."

He was clutching her personal belongings to his chest, his head hanging.

That handmade flier for Haruka Seta. All this time, Morimine has had a burning obsession with this case, even as he condemned the police. And when I showed him the flier, he said: 'That takes me back.'"

All of this led Amon to one answer.

Morimine opened a cute, girlish notebook he'd found in the box, and a photograph fell out. It was an old photo but there was no doubt: the photograph was of Haruka Seta and Morimine, standing close together.

"Amon! Morimine!"

Investigators and police officers burst into the Utsumi house, which was suddenly chaotic.

When Yanagi finally rushed in and found Tojo, he ran over and gave him a slap on the head without breaking his stride.

"What is wrong with you?!"

"S-sorry..."

Tojo was almost in tears. Morimine cut in between them.

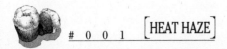

"Wait, wait, wait," he said. "We only came in here because of Tojo, and what's more, he's the one who finished this Ghoul off. Right, Tojo?"

"Uh . . . yeah."

"Huh? Did you say Tojo did this?"

Morimine had offered Tojo a lifeline. And he wasn't lying, either. Amon gave a nod in agreement to Yanagi, who was torn between belief and doubt. His expression was complicated, and he sighed.

"But what happened, Tojo? Your Quinque is broken. It doesn't look like you'll ever be able to use it again," Yanagi said.

Knowing he couldn't tell Yanagi that a Ghoul had used his Quinque as a shield, Tojo's face looked drawn.

"Forget that, Yanagi. We don't know the whereabouts of Otokaze, the lady in her fifties who was the housekeeper here. She looked after Koharu Utsumi, who was a Ghoul, so there's a strong possibility that she's a Ghoul too."

"Right, got it. I'll get an emergency search going."

"And we also need to investigate Koharu's adoptive father."

"Okay, okay. To think that . . . she was a Ghoul. And I didn't see it at all. I've still got a lot to learn."

Then, asking Yanagi to take over, Amon and Morimine left the scene.

"I'll take you back to the CCG," Morimine said, but when they got into his car they both went silent.

As he drove, Morimine's expression was the same as always. But the look of pain on his face earlier was burned into Amon's mind.

"What the hell are you staring at?"

Amon had been looking at him without realizing it. "Sorry," he said, looking away.

"She was my girlfriend," Morimine said with a little smile. "We went together that night to watch the fireworks. It was a long way home for her, so I offered to take her home, but she told me she'd be fine . . . That was the last time I saw her."

Amon didn't know what to say.

"The police barely investigated it. That's why I became a policeman. I thought that once I was a cop I'd find out what happened to her. A childish idea. I wanted to find the guy who did this and kill them."

I wonder if he feels like he did that today. If it might give him a measure of peace. But there's nothing gleeful about the way he looks right now.

"But, you know, when I got to be a cop, I realized something. Vengeance or revenge or whatever is for idiots. There are just so many reasons why people commit crimes. And if you go way back, maybe they were hurt by someone, maybe they were tormented, you know, it all goes back to reasons like that. Those kinds of negative emotions become a driving force and it just causes more pain for those around them."

Morimine gripped the steering wheel tightly.

"When I saw that the hatred I had might drive me to hurt someone one day, it scared me. I thought I had to catch criminals in order to break the cycle of evil. But now, I . . ." He went quiet. After a long

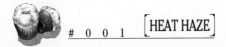

0 0 1   [HEAT HAZE]

silence, he spoke again, putting emphasis on every word. "Now, I can't help but pity them. Even her."

Amon looked at him again.

"I mean, if I'd been born a Ghoul, what would I do?" Morimine said. Then he apologized. "Sorry, I guess I shouldn't say that to a Ghoul investigator," he added, and stopped talking.

Amon thought to himself. About whether they had seen all of the personal effects of the girls that Koharu had taken. He wondered if Morimine had remembered that notebook that had belonged to Haruka Seta, the one that the photograph had fallen out of.

Perhaps, when Morimine had taken her statement that time, Koharu had realized that this guilt-tormented man was the right age, and maybe that's why she put that barrette in front of the police station. Maybe she wanted him to catch her, to break the cycle of evil.

VII

Once the report on Koharu Utsumi was done, a replacement for Amon was assigned and his work in the 8th Ward was over.

"Amon! We heard you found and destroyed a Ghoul who wasn't even suspected of being one!"

When he returned to the 20th Ward, Seido Takizawa came over to talk to him in a state of excitement. *Where'd he hear that?*

"No, it was all thanks to the cooperation of the police."

"Don't be so humble! You put an end to the deaths of young girls, targeted and eaten in such a despicable, ghoulish way. You're amazing!" rambled Takizawa, his fist clenched.

He's so happy you'd think he'd done it himself.

"Nice work, Kotaro." It was Kosuke Hoji, a gentle man from the Combat Division, who next came to thank him.

"Yanagi's been talking you up, you know. If you hadn't been so attentive he could've been the one to save all those people." That praise from Hoji, an associate special investigator, punched Amon in the gut.

"Thank you all," he said, and bowed. But then he realized that one person was missing from the scene.

"Where's Juzo?"

He didn't see Juzo Suzuya, who had his own special way of getting at people.

"Oh, he's at Shinohara's."

"Really?"

"Yeah. Since Shinohara is injured he can't give hands-on education, so he's drilling Suzuya from bed."

Juzo was not an Academy graduate, and he had problems with his temperament, meaning he was woefully lacking in some of the knowledge an investigator needed.

Shinohara had been confined to bed since being injured in the Aogiri battle, but he was still finding things he could reasonably do and continuing to teach. *He's an example to us all.*

"Next, about the Rabbit case . . ."

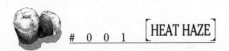 # 0 0 1 [HEAT HAZE]

"Have you made progress?!"

Hoji shook his head apologetically. "No, actually, there's been no news since the incident. It's almost scary how quiet it's been," he said.

"Oh . . . I see."

When Amon got to his desk, it was covered in reports and documents that had piled up while he'd been gone. He went through them all, catching up on what had happened while he'd been away.

The results of Koharu's autopsy confirmed that the Ghoul-specific bodily fluids left on Mai's barrette belonged to her. And the bones and hair they'd found had allowed them to identify her victims—without a doubt, she had killed all the girls who had gone missing.

But Koharu's adoptive father, Yujiro Utsumi, was still in intensive care and his condition was deteriorating, meaning that he was in no state for an interview. Otokaze was still missing too. And the identity of the man who had been blackmailing Koharu was still unknown.

Beyond a doubt, Koharu had been kidnapping girls and eating them, but Amon still felt a dark cloud over him that he couldn't quite dispel.

"I hope the future . . . that you want . . . comes to pass."

Tears streamed down her cheeks, falling from her red eyes. Unexpected words from a Ghoul. They remind me of the tears I saw from the Ghoul with the eye patch crying that day.

"Please . . . don't kill me."

Amon set aside his work and went over to the window, looking down at the tree-lined street below.

Fiendish Ghouls wearing masks are perverting this world. That's undeniable. But is there really only one version of the truth?

When I told him I was going back to the 20th Ward, Morimine said: "Koharu Utsumi might've been a Ghoul, but I don't think she's the only one to blame in those cases, if you see what I mean. So I'm gonna find out what happened." Then he added, "Let me know if there's anything else I can help you with," and laughed.

It was hard for Amon to understand how a man who'd had someone so important to him taken away could think like that. But he didn't think Morimine's outlook on life was wrong either.

I've got to talk to the Ghoul with the eye patch. The thought now filled Amon's mind. *If I can talk to him, I might see something I haven't been able to before.*

"I will find him . . ."

Amon gave his face a little slap and returned to his duties. *Because there's no time for stalling.*

[EMBROIDERY]

Spin and spun, the hempen thread
stitched and stitched and tied at the end.

There were few streetlights to cast aside the dark of night on this side street not too far from downtown. On one corner, right next to one of the trees that lined the roadside, was a street vendor whose features were hidden beneath a hood. Set out in front of the proprietor was an assortment of masks, their designs all strikingly unique, unusual enough to get passersby to stop and stare, but none took it upon themselves to purchase one.

"Hey, that's kinda neat," said the latest customer, stopping to look at one such mask before just as quickly turning to move on. "It's impressive, but who'd wear something like that?" As he went to leave, however, he was startled by the stallkeeper's voice calling out through the darkness.

"Hey! What did you say just now?"

The passerby let out a short, startled gasp and went wide-eyed as the stallkeeper stood up, eliciting a louder cry of shock as the hood drew back to reveal garish blond hair and flashy piercings. The threatening and ill-bred demeanor marked the stallkeeper as a young thug, and the customer bolted off in a panic at the very sight.

"Bah. What a wuss," muttered the stallkeeper, pulling the hood up and sitting back down in irritation. "Dammit. If he'd just take me on as his apprentice, then—"

A new arrival broke that train of thought.

"Could I have a moment, miss?"

She was somewhat surprised to be called "miss," given her mannish facial features and body devoid of any real feminine curves. That, along with her height of over 170 centimeters and her rough disposition, led to her frequently be mistaken for a man.

She looked up to see a man in an unkempt suit, probably in his mid-30s, hunkered down and regarding her face keenly.

"Actually, let me be up-front with you," he said, taking out a police notebook.

As soon as she saw it, the stallkeeper braced herself to dart off, just like the customer had earlier. The detective must have seen him run off screaming as he had, or maybe he'd noticed that she was operating a stall without a permit.

"No, no, it's not like that," the detective said. "I'd like to ask you about masks. Could I, ah, have your name, miss?"

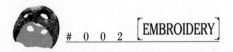

0 0 2 [EMBROIDERY]

"You're really not gonna try and arrest me?"

"Nah. This isn't my jurisdiction. The name's Morimine. I'm a detective from the 8th Ward. The 23rd Ward's outside my beat."

Bordered on one side by the river and on another by the sea, the 23rd Ward was adjacent to the 8th Ward. The detective who'd introduced himself as Morimine was waiting intently for a response. Still holding on to her suspicions, the stallkeeper answered hesitantly.

"I'm Asa," she offered, giving at least her name. "So, what did you wanna ask about?"

Morimine produced a photograph in turn. The picture showed a leather mask adorned with fine embroidery. It was simple, but a single look was enough to make the sheer degree of craftsmanship possessed by its creator obvious. Asa was unexpectedly impressed, her gaze fiercely drawn to it.

"I'm looking for the person who made this mask. Do you have any thoughts as to who it might be?"

"This? I mean I can tell it's not one of mine. Beyond that..." It didn't appear to be the work of the mask maker Asa so revered, either. That being the case, she didn't have the information Morimine was after, but she did now have an interest in this mask.

"Hey, mind if I borrow this picture?" she asked.

"Borrow it? Why?"

"Because if I check with some other mask maskers, maybe they'll know something! I mean, right?"

Morimine mulled it over for a bit. "All right," he said, handing the photograph over.

"Okay then. If I find anything out, I'll give the police a call."

"Much obliged," Morimine said, bowing his head. "Any information you can find, no matter how trivial, would be greatly appreciated."

Morimine's face was all business, but Asa merely gave him a quick, "All right," before turning away.

Behind her, she heard the detective mutter to himself, presumably thinking he wouldn't be overheard. "Guess this case still isn't over . . ."

"As if I'd ever get in touch with the cops! Your little photograph's all mine, now, dumbass!" Asa laughed as soon as Morimine and any other bystanders were out of sight, her attention fixed on the picture, a complacent smile on her face. "Still, he oughta be grateful."

Asa ground her molars tightly together. Several seconds later, power coursed through her body, her eyes turning red as she stared at the photograph. She licked her lips, pushed off the ground with a kick, and a moment later was atop the nearby roof. "After all, I *did* let him leave without eating him!"

Standing at the top of the food chain, feared by humanity for their special abilities, were Ghouls—and Asa was one among their number.

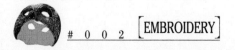 # 0 0 2 [EMBROIDERY]

II

Back in the 4th Ward, her old hometown, Asa left the train
station and wove her way between the buildings, through narrow
streets, making her way farther and farther in until she arrived at the
mask shop HySy Art Mask Studio. The store's logo was emblazoned
on the wall outside, masks peering out through the windows. The
very sight stirred Asa's excitement, and somehow instilled in her a
sense of pride.

"Howdy!" she called out as she knocked on the door, and when
she stepped inside, one of the mannequin heads fitted with a mask
caught her eye. "Whoa! This's a new one! Oh, wow, this is *beyond*
fine! This is beyond *amazing*!"

She had meant to exchange pleasantries first, but unable to resist the allure of the mask, scurried right on over to it.

"Same as always I see, Asa," came a leisurely voice from farther back in the shop.

"Ah! S-sorry! Guess I sorta spaced out, there..." She turned around to see a man staring back at her from the workshop.

"Uh-huh. Been a while." The man sported countless piercings and was tattooed all the way down to his fingertips. He was Uta, who once had reigned over the 4th Ward. He'd since been driven from that position of leadership, and now put his manual dexterity to use to get by running a mask shop.

Asa had been a little girl when Uta ran the ward, but she'd always admired his aura of sheer strength. She was further enamored of the masks he fashioned, and she resolved to one day have a mask shop just like his.

"You masks really are awesome, Uta! Please take me on as your apprentice!" Asa got down and prostrated herself before him. "I beg you!" she said, lowering her head.

"Our styles are too different, Asa."

Time and again, Asa had come to Uta and begged to be his apprentice like this, only for him to calmly refuse her.

"How's the 23rd Ward? I hear things are pretty rough there right now."

The change in subject told Asa that it was a no-go this time as well, and she bit her lip as she stood back up. "Cochlea was attacked, and things have been a mess because of it. The doves are swarming

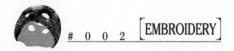

0 0 2 [EMBROIDERY]

all over the place. Heck, same goes for the pain-in-the-ass Ghouls who broke out. I hear there are lots of Ghouls who're refugees from other wards too."

As a matter of propriety, Asa couldn't open a shop in the 4th Ward, where Uta dwelled, so she'd settled in the 23rd Ward, which was now embroiled in strife. Rather than seeing their brethren as having been liberated from their human captors, the Ghouls of the 23rd Ward resented them more than anything else.

"Lately I've been considering moving to another ward until the situation there dies down. But enough about me! I actually came because I wanted to ask you something, Uta." She handed over the photo she'd gotten from the detective.

"What's this?"

"Some detective came to ask me about it today. Do you recognize this mask?"

The reflection of the mask in the photo was visible in Uta's eyes. "A policeman? Not a Ghoul investigator?"

"Yeah. I guess he was on some sort of case. But anyway, isn't it super pretty? Who could've made something like that?"

Asa had a hard time reading Uta's face; he was always placid and calm, ever composed and unwavering. She regarded him casually for a few seconds, his thoughts a mystery to her, before he put away the tools on his workbench and stood up. He slipped on the coat that hung next to him and donned his hat.

"Uta? You goin' out somewhere?"

"Yeah. Think I got a little hunch."

"A hunch? Wait . . . Uta, you think you know who the crafter of this mask might be?!"

As Asa brimmed with excitement, Uta stepped out of the shop and flipped the door sign to Closed as he said, "Not quite a crafter, per se. Tsumugi used to make masks. And I know a place where she was a regular customer."

"Tsumugi . . ." So that was the mask maker's name. Asa was growing more and more curious about what sort of person she could be. "Would it, ah, be all right for me to go with you? I'd love to see her work in person!"

Asa clenched her fists in fierce anticipation. "You're the one who came to me to do the talking," Uta said to her. "It's all you."

Uta took Asa to a café in the 20th Ward called Anteiku.

"Hey, I know this place. Doesn't Yomo work here?" she asked. Renji Yomo was one of the many Ghouls who'd mysteriously shown up back when Uta ran the 4th Ward.

"Yeah. But we're not here for Renji today. We're just here to see the owner."

The café looked to already be closed for the evening, the lights all off, but when Uta rang the bell, an elderly, white-haired man showed up. "Uta? Well, this is a rare sight. What's going on?"

"Sorry to show up so late, Yoshimura, but there's something I wanted to ask you about, if you don't mind."

A kindly smile curled Yoshimura's lips as Uta spoke so politely to him. He was an older man, but one who gave off a sense of unfathomable power. Noticing Asa, he asked, "Who's this?"

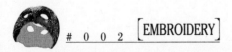

0 0 2 [EMBROIDERY]

"Oh! I'm Asa, Uta's prospective apprentice."

Uta neither confirmed nor denied Asa's casual assertion. Yoshimura narrowed his eyes at her as she felt her dejection set in yet again. "Well, come on in, at least," he said, waving them into the shop.

"How's your health?" Uta asked.

"Need to take it easy. Can't really leave the café, but otherwise well enough."

Yoshimura fetched them some coffee as they took seats at the counter. Asa had never been to a café like this one, but the luxuriant aroma rising from her coffee cup was enough to tell her it was of topmost quality.

"So, what's going on?"

Uta took out the photograph. "The police are looking for whoever made this mask. I think it may have been Tsumugi."

Yoshimura furrowed his brow. "If something like this is making the rounds, I suppose that means something happened to 'him.'"

"Has Tsumugi been by here recently?"

"No. I'd been on a break from working the café for a while, but I haven't seen her."

The conversation went on, the others ignoring Asa as she struggled to follow what they were talking about. Without much else to do, she sipped her coffee and looked around the café. The place had quite the subdued atmosphere for an establishment run by Ghouls. They probably got a lot of human customers as well. That made Asa somewhat jealous.

"He may have been neglecting his other info-gathering duties because he's been caught up with that other thing. I'll look into it," Yoshimura said.

"All right. I'll go check up on Tsumugi then."

The conversation seemed to have wrapped up. Seeing Uta get to his feet, Asa hurriedly followed after him. "Uta, what are we doing next?"

"I'm going to Tsumugi's house. She's here in the 20th Ward, so it's not far."

Soon Asa would be face-to-face with this Tsumugi. Would she have the sullen demeanor of a Ghoul artisan? Or would she possess the refined beauty that she'd conveyed through her mask? Asa could feel the anticipation blossoming within her.

"This place?"

Unlike Anteiku, where Uta had taken her just previously, there were few people roaming the streets here on the outskirts of town. The small, old, Western-style house looked like it could easily have been haunted.

Uta knocked on the door, but there was no response from within.

"Guess she's not home."

"No, I think she is," Uta said, and true to his words, Asa soon felt someone approaching from inside the house. She swallowed a breath and waited.

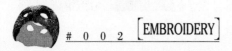 # 0 0 2 [EMBROIDERY]

At last, the door opened, revealing—

"What's with you, old lady?" Asa blurted. She was an elderly woman, probably in her eighties, her face crisscrossed with wrinkles and her back hunched. She gave off none of the same menace Yoshimura had, and her scent was human. "What are you, the housekeeper or something? We're here for Tsumugi. Go get her for us."

How dare this dirty old hag impose upon them so? Asa was dejected, but in response to her slights, the old woman said, "Yes, I am Tsumugi."

"Huh?" Asa's train of thought was momentarily broken. She turned to Uta. "No, this can't be . . ."

"Tsumugi Yamagata. She's a seamstress," Uta said, introducing the old woman.

"Whaaat? You're telling me this little old witch of a lady made that mask?"

Tsumugi's expression remained unchanged despite Asa's rude words. "At least a witch would be far more charming than you Ghouls," she replied.

Her reply had a more troubling connotation, though. "Oh, you old hag..."

She'd been able to see that they were Ghouls. Asa glared at Tsumugi warily, but the woman simply muttered, "Doesn't make much difference to me either way," before turning her gaze to Uta. "You don't usually come all the way out here. Is it about something I made, like the girl says?"

"Yes," Uta replied.

Tsumugi looked back and forth between the pair of them. "Come in," she told them, welcoming them inside.

The doorway opened up into a large lobby. Despite the house's ostentatious appearance from the outside, the interior was rather Spartan. The living room the woman led them to had only the bare minimum of furnishings.

"Now, what's all this about, then?" Tsumugi asked as she sat down on the sofa, facing her visitors.

"Right here... This is one of your masks, right?" Uta asked.

Tsumugi put on a pair of reading glasses and inspected the photo she'd been handed. "Yes, I'm sure of it. This is one of mine. What are you doing with this picture, though?"

"Apparently the police are searching for whoever made

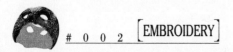 # 0 0 2 [EMBROIDERY]

this mask."

"The police?" Tsumugi raised an eyebrow. "Hmph . . . I see. And so that's why you're here." She nodded in understanding, her body sinking farther into the sofa. "Well, this changes nothing. Now, if you'd be so kind as to not let your silly suspicions run wild."

Asa didn't quite know what was going on, but she could tell Uta had come here out of concern for Tsumugi, and to see the older woman rebuff that thoughtfulness ticked Asa right off.

"Hey now, you old bag! I don't know what your deal is, but Uta came all this way for you. What's with the attitude?" She rose to her feet threateningly.

But Tsumugi paid Asa no heed, and tossed the photograph back dismissively. "If that's all, then I'd like you to leave now."

"Listen, you damn hag, I—"

"It's all right, Asa."

Uta's words cut off any further complaint, but Asa still rankled inwardly, clenching her jaw in frustration. Uta gave her a look before turning his attention back to Tsumugi and broaching a new subject. "Actually, there was one other thing I came for."

"Yes?"

"I'd like to try decorating my next mask with some embroidery. I'd appreciate it if you'd show me your design sketches and needle-work samples. A look at quality work might give me some good ideas."

Asa blinked at that. She'd had no idea Uta was considering anything of the sort. Tsumugi raised an eyebrow, apparently just as surprised, her gaze wandering about as she seemed to consider it.

Finally, with a disgusted sigh, she replied, "Embroidery wouldn't suit your disgusting masks."

Asa trailed a bit behind Uta after they left Tsumugi's manor. "So you've been planning on doing some embroidery?" she asked.

"Yeah. There've been some masks that I thought would look good with that sort of thing."

"So then are you going to be going back to that old lady's house?"

"I suppose it wouldn't hurt to stretch my legs if I wanted her to check my needlework."

It was rare for Uta to adorn his masks with needlework, but Asa was curious to see what sort of things could be made with that process. She looked back at Tsumugi's house, and made a decision for herself.

III

The next day, Asa went back alone, steeling herself as she knocked on the manor door. When there came no response, she knocked harder.

This time, Tsumugi's annoyed visage revealed itself. "Yeah? What do you want?"

"Is Uta there?" Asa asked, poking her head in through the open door to look farther inside.

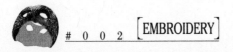

0 0 2 [EMBROIDERY]

"Is that Asa? What's going on?"

"Uta!" she called out, and he looked up at her from the living room as she got his attention. "I, ah, figured I might as well try my hand at some embroidery too! Would it be all right for me to join you?"

In response, Uta said, "You'll have to ask Tsumugi."

Apparently she wasn't going to be able to just ignore Tsumugi's presence. "Hey, old bag. Lemme join in." She folded her arms, demanding instead of asking, in no mood to kowtow to a human, let alone an old lady like her.

Tsumugi shrugged ambivalently and said, "Don't make a mess."

Asa's face lit up, and she scooted past Tsumugi to make her way over to Uta. He was at a large table in the living room, seemingly looking over Tsumugi's design sketches, some of which jumped right out at Asa.

These were polished designs, and Asa was so overwhelmed by their beauty that the sight of them stopped her in her tracks.

"Pretty, eh?" Uta murmured.

The words snapped Asa out of her reverie. "Well, yours are even more amazing!" she said on reflex.

"What would an amateur brat like you know?"

Asa turned to look at Tsumugi, sitting on the sofa behind her. "I'm not an amateur!" she snapped, a competitive impulse blazing to the fore.

Tsumugi glared at her. "You're a mask maker, too?" she asked.

"I am. And here's proof!" Asa said, reaching into her bag

95

and pulling out one of the masks she'd made, holding it up to show Tsumugi.

Tsumugi narrowed her eyes to look at the mask before snorting out a nasal laugh. "What's this? Your stitching is loose, and your sense of symmetry is poor. And did you *try* to stretch out the fabric this much? Look how it's all warped. You messed up your measurements and then tried to compensate afterward, didn't you? What a cheap-looking piece of junk."

"H-hey now, you old bag! My mask making is . . ." But Asa's rebuttal didn't come. Tsumugi's words had hit too close to home. Instead, she spit out an annoyed, "Just shut up, you hag."

Ignoring Asa's angry outburst, Tsumugi scrutinized the mask carefully as she laid out a sheet of paper. She then began to briskly sketch something. Asa tried to get a better look, and saw that Tsumugi was putting together a pattern for Asa's mask going by sight alone. Moreover, it was a simpler and more refined pattern than the one Asa had used when she'd made the mask herself.

"Whoa, how'd you do that?" Asa picked up the sheet of paper, curious as to how Tsumugi had been able to identify all her mask's flaws. Tsumugi set her pencil against her chin and turned away with a huff.

"This old hag's a real pain in the ass, Uta," Asa said, hoping for some backup, but Uta was engrossed in the design sketches. Ideas were probably blossoming in his mind right now. Tsumugi stood bolt upright to stop the interruption, and she tossed something to Asa.

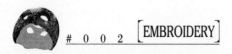 # 0 0 2 [EMBROIDERY]

"Huh?" Asa looked in her hands to see a scrap of cloth. "What's this for?"

"If you've got the time, you can help me with some cutting. I'll even pay you a small sum."

Asa's face contorted in confusion at the sudden proposal. "Huh? Why should I have to work under some old bag like you?"

"What, are you scared that I'll see that you're not as good as your dear Uta?" Tsumugi said as Asa was about to toss the scrap of cloth right back at her.

Asa bristled at being called out, but merely snapped back, "Fine, I'll do it! It might even be fun."

Several hours later, Asa had grown weary of the boredom and the repeated drudge work. "How come I've gotta do like fifty rows of backstitching? What are you even going to use this cloth for, anyway?"

"Your impatience is what makes your work so crude. Now be quiet and work with your hands, not your mouth. I won't accept sloppy work from you."

Asa was ready to throw in the towel then and there, but a casual "Hang in there, Asa!" from Uta kept her from bailing. She reminded herself that she was here to see Uta's workmanship in action, and so she'd find some way to get through this work.

The day wore on until it got dark, and Tsumugi stood up. "That time already, huh . . ."

"What, you goin' to bed already? Man, you old folks really do turn in early," Asa scoffed.

"Fool," Tsumugi replied. "I'm going to do some shopping."

Well, at any rate, this meant Asa was free of Tsumugi's boring busywork now. As that thought was setting in, however, Uta looked up. "Let me go with you," he said, getting to his feet as well.

"You're going with her, Uta?"

"Yeah. Could use a breather."

Well, that changed things a bit. Asa glared over at Tsumugi and called out, "I'm going too then!"

After they got outside, Uta said, "I've got a lot to think about, so I'll walk farther behind." He then let himself drop back. He probably wanted to flesh out the designs he had in mind. Asa wanted to walk alongside him, but she might wind up distracting him, and so without much other choice, she fell into step alongside Tsumugi.

"So where are we going, old lady?" Asa asked, realizing she didn't know where they were even heading yet.

"The market district," Tsumugi replied. "We humans get our food by going out and buying it, unlike your kind."

That was right: Tsumugi knew Asa was a Ghoul. That being the case, Asa pressed the subject. "How come you're not scared of us, old lady? You're not worried about getting eaten?"

"Would *you* want to eat the flesh of a shriveled old woman? Besides, I've been dealing with Ghouls for a long time, starting with Uta."

"But he might have a change of heart and kill you. You *are* pretty aggravating, after all." Asa reached out and threateningly grabbed the old woman's neck from behind, but Tsumugi simply

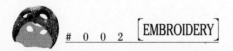

[EMBROIDERY]

slapped her hand away.

"I trust Uta," she said. "It would be uncouth for me to doubt the people he keeps company with."

The old woman seemed pretty indifferent toward Uta, but apparently they had some foundation of trust in their relationship that Asa couldn't see. Asa snuck a look back at Uta, then asked Tsumugi, more quietly this time, "Are you and Uta close friends?"

"Hmm. I'm not sure. I do appreciate his craft, though."

"I know, right? Uta's such an incredible mask masker!" Asa was pleased to hear Uta complimented so, her expression suddenly brightening up, but she then hurriedly wiped that look off her face when she remembered she was dealing with Tsumugi.

"You really do look up to him, don't you?"

"Of course I do. Lots of us in the 4th Ward do."

"I'll bet."

Asa continued to hang out with Tsumugi as they made their way through the market district, walking around for roughly two hours. They checked out grocer's stalls and fishmongers that Asa would never have needed to be anywhere near if she'd been with another Ghoul, which left her feeling groggy.

"I can't believe you seriously eat grass and fish and stuff," Asa grumbled as she smelled the odor of fish coming from the kitchen. They were back at Tsumugi's house now, and Asa had been given the tedious task of covering her cloth with backstitching. "Let things that grow in the dirt stay there and leave things that swim back in the ocean."

"Still," Uta pointed out, "A human meal is kind of like a colorful work of art."

"Why would you want to put art in your mouth?" Asa asked, scrunching up her face at that. "When *my* food's got a weird color, I . . ."

Tsumugi came out with a tray loaded with food. The smell was even stronger now, and Asa unwittingly pinched her nose shut on reflex, but after getting a quick, narrow-eyed glance at Tsumugi's food, her hand came away from her face. As Uta had said, Tsumugi's meal came in lovely bowls and piled atop plates, the many bright colors a feast for the eyes. It was an interesting thing to view as art. Once Tsumugi started eating, the sight struck Asa as grotesque and unsettling, but she felt a fresh surge of joy at having learned something new.

And I bet Uta has learned a lot about me that he didn't know before too.

That thought made her somewhat lonesome. She couldn't shake the feeling that no matter how she tried to chase after him, she could never catch up.

That night, after Uta had gone back to his shop, Asa was alone in Tsumugi's living room, continuing to work on her backstitching. Half the reason was that she was determined to actually finish the job, but the other half was that she was starting to find the simple work a little bit fun.

"What? You're still here?"

The voice made Asa look up. Tsumugi was standing there, dressed for bed.

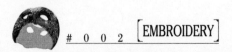 # 0 0 2 [EMBROIDERY]

"You're the one who told me to do this!" Asa snapped. "So I'm not going until it's finished!"

Tsumugi said nothing in reply, and instead sat down right next to her on the sofa. She watched Asa for a while, keeping her thoughts to herself, and then got her sewing equipment from the shelf and began some embroidery.

"You don't need to head back home?" she asked.

"Don't got one. Selling masks doesn't bring in a ton of money. For someone like me, it's basically like being a part-time day laborer."

"What about your parents?"

"My mother was already gone as far back as I remember. My dad was an idiot and got killed after he picked a fight with some other Ghouls."

Asa was unconcerned with her own past, and her tone showed it. "I see . . ." Tsumugi murmured in response before going silent.

That silence continued for a while before Asa found it too stifling. She looked up to see a bit of Tsumugi's needlework. "What's that?"

"Oh, this? Keeping my hands active helps me stay sharp." Tsumugi then unfurled a scarf embroidered in silver.

"Whoa, that's amazing!" It was somewhat irritating that Tsumugi's handiwork impressed Asa as much as it did, but she couldn't quash the emotional response she had. The scarf sported a large ring of flowers with expanding leaves, all of it bordered by a beautiful curving ivy pattern. The needlework reminded Asa of the adorned mask in the photo she'd gotten from the detective.

"So you really did make that mask, huh?" For the first time since coming here, Asa could truly believe that.

"Well, I'm originally a dressmaker by trade, so my masks have mostly been special orders from my regular clients."

That limited the possibilities of who had owned this mask to a very small pool of people. "So hey, old lady. How come the police had a photo of one of your masks?" Asa asked, curious. "I could tell that Uta was worried about you too. Is that mask dangerous somehow?"

Tsumugi set her embroidery work on her knee and stared into the distance, her eyes narrowing. Asa, who before now had been short-tempered and snappish with her, found herself waiting calmly for a response.

"I made that mask on the request of a very wealthy individual," Tsumugi muttered. "He had it made for a Ghoul."

"If it's a Ghoul mask, why are the police involved? Isn't this usually Ghoul investigator business?"

Tsumugi let out a deep sigh of consternation. "That detective must have good instincts. I suppose Uta is worried that I'll be in a risky predicament if it's discovered I made a mask for a Ghoul."

"Ah, I see. You'd be marked as a Ghoul collaborator, then?" Asa asked, at last getting a handle on the situation.

"Those masks are a Ghoul's way of keeping hidden. If it was found out that I'd abetted one by making a mask, I'd be brought up on charges."

"So the mask *is* dangerous, then. If this detective finds you he's

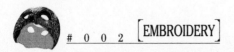

0 0 2 [EMBROIDERY]

probably going to arrest you."

"I'm just an old woman without much time left. What point would there be in arresting me?" Tsumugi replied, her tone unconcerned, her face showing some deep forethought.

"You're ready, then? Is that it?"

"Hmm?"

"I just . . . sometimes I get the same sort of impression from Uta." A willingness to take on anything and everything, come what may. Even an outsider was capable of seeing it. "Now that I think about it, if anything happened, someone might be able to track Uta's creations back to him too. And he still makes what he does, despite all the risks?"

Things weren't like that for Asa. As someone who lived from day to day thanks to her street stall, if something bad happened to her she could just run. Running a shop and selling merchandise meant walking a fine line. One that Uta, as well as Tsumugi, continued to walk.

"What's got you so sentimental all of a sudden?" Tsumugi asked, looking at Asa and sounding rather perplexed.

"I wouldn't say I'm being sentimental as much as . . ."

"You're an easy one to read, girl. Here, use this to blow your nose," Tsumugi said, tossing the embroidered scarf to Asa.

"Hey! My noise isn't running! And even if it were, I couldn't blow my nose with this!"

"Well, she's got some spirit, after all. If you need to take a break from your work, you can sleep on the sofa. You can finish up the rest in the morning. Don't cut any corners." Tsumugi groaned as she stood up and then returned to her own room.

"Oh come on, where does she get off?" Asa grumbled as she took a look at Tsumugi's embroidery work, letting out a gasp of astonishment.

"This is incredible . . ."

IV

After that, Asa began making her way over to Tsumugi's house daily. She hoped to see Uta during her visits, of course, but even on days when he wasn't there, she would stay and work quietly in the living room.

There were few passersby here on the edge of town, with the sound of birds chirping the only real thing to hear. Asa, who before had been forced to always work out in the elements, was now able to muster up some concentration. She might even be able to correct her shortcomings, fixing shoddy workmanship she had rushed to complete before.

No one came to visit, however, and Asa wondered whether the poor old woman had any friends or family.

"Hey, is it time to go shopping?"

"Yes. I'm in the mood for fish today."

"Urgh."

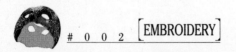 # 0 0 2 [EMBROIDERY]

Around when the sun was going down, Tsumugi started getting ready to go out. Asa could have continued with her remaining work, but decided to accompany the old woman, figuring she could use a bit of a break. They were heading to the nearby market district again today. Tsumugi stopped by the fishmonger's, poring about for things to make dinner with.

"You sure do eat fish a lot," Asa called out as she hurried to catch up. She had been at the general store across the way, looking for materials she might use in mask making, but Tsumugi now seemed to have finished her purchase and was now heading to another shop.

"Oh, well if it isn't Tsumugi! Long time no see!"

The sound of a woman's high-pitched voice stopped Asa in her tracks. She looked to see an old woman around Tsumugi's age, with her daughter and grandson in tow. "What's up? You know this lady?"

It appeared that this was indeed one of Tsumugi's human acquaintances. Asa was about to go back to the general store so as not to be a bother when she heard the other woman speak again. "How are you doing nowadays? Living on your own, I take it?" Asa felt an edge of malice in those words, and so she stayed put.

"Yes, I'm getting by on my own."

"Oh my! Being alone at our age must be dreadful!" The woman spoke with exaggerated sympathy, her face awash with an air of superiority. "And you used to be so pretty, with so many admirers, too! But I suppose while having a wealthy lover can let you live in luxury, it doesn't bless you with a family. I suppose it's providence to be cast aside after one's beauty fades!" The woman looked at her own grandson and daughter, then let out a haughty laugh. "It's far better to simply be ordinary. I get to live out my days with my family, surrounded by their warmth. I just wanted you to understand that."

Hearing that, Asa felt an indignation growing inside her. She was about to step in and knock the woman out with a single punch before thinking better of it. Humans had their own form of social etiquette, and if an outsider came in to unilaterally break those rules, it would not only bring harm onto her for being a Ghoul, but onto Tsumugi as well.

As she stood in frustrated silence, smoke nearly coming out of her ears as she thought about to do, she caught sight of herself reflected in the general store's display window. "Ah." And that's when she got an idea.

"But anyway, I am in the middle of shopping here, so if you'll pardon me," said the woman, her voice laced with sarcasm.

She was about to leave with her family when Asa called out in a low voice. "Tsumugi!" she said, her tone nice and familiar. "There you are! I've been looking all over for you. How could you just leave me behind like that?"

Asa could feel herself getting goosebumps as she spoke, and Tsumugi was uncharacteristically caught off guard. The other woman's eyes went wide in disbelief. "Oh, don't try to carry all this by yourself. Let me give you a hand," Asa said with a smile as she went to help Tsumugi with her bags.

"W-w-wait, Tsumugi, who is this young man?" the woman asked, mistaking Asa for a boy, just as Asa had anticipated.

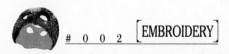

The smile never left Asa's face as she said, "You'd better not be bad-mouthing my Tsumugi, you old hag."

The other woman was dumbstruck, her family in something of a panic alongside her, as Asa snugged one arm around Tsumugi's shoulder and marched off.

"What was that all about? Oh, I've got goose-bumps," Tsumugi said after they'd left the market district and were out of ear-shot of any passersby.

Asa withdrew her hand from Tsumugi's shoul-der. "Do I gross you out that much?" she snapped. For a moment, there was an awkward silence, but then Asa mustered herself to broach the subject that

had come up earlier. "So, you used to have a lover, huh? That's pretty amazing for an old lady like you."

"Every old lady was young once, you know."

"Oh yeah?" Asa said. She had a hard time imagining Tsumugi ever being young. "So what was this person like? Some old guy?"

"No, he was younger than me. Well, I suppose he's an old man by this point. I haven't seen him in some time."

"Wait, you two aren't still together, are you?"

"Don't be ridiculous," Tsumugi snorted in reply. "This was when we were younger. Nowadays we're friends, of a sort. We see each other around once a year, maybe. It just seems that nearly everything that happens makes me think of him. Bah."

Asa found herself at a loss for words at the sullen look on Tsumugi's face. Her expression reverted back to normal soon enough, however. "Anyhow, give me back my bags. I know you hate the smell," she said, extending a wrinkly hand.

"It's no big deal. I can handle it," Asa replied curtly.

"Yeah?" Tsumugi said. She then looked up, as if having just remembered something. "But anyway . . ."

"Hmm? What?"

"The look on that woman's face when you came by and scared her out of her wits was spectacular," Tsumugi snickered.

Asa looked back at her and laughed. "Wasn't it just?"

That evening, after Tsumugi had finished eating dinner, there came a knock at the door. "Uta!" Asa called out, sensing his presence, and she hurried to the doorway. However, when she opened

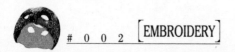

0 0 2 [EMBROIDERY]

the door, she that Uta wasn't alone.

"Y-Yomo..."

At Uta's side was Renji Yomo, Yoshimura's current right-hand man. He gave Asa a brief look, then turned his gaze farther inside.

"What, is Yoshimura trying to butt in on things?" Asa said.

Tsumugi showed up, almost as if in response to Asa's puzzled tone. That's right—Tsumugi was a regular customer at Anteiku, wasn't she?

Yomo looked at Asa, and then spoke matter-of-factly. "Yujiro Utsumi has fallen ill and is in a hospital in the 8th Ward. He doesn't have long."

Yujiro Utsumi. It wasn't a name Asa had heard before. Tsumugi, on the other hand, raised an eyebrow. "I expected as much," she said. "Then Koharu is..."

Yomo said nothing.

Despite the lack of response, Tsumugi seemed to know all she needed to. "I see..."

"Uh, old lady?"

"Sorry, but my hands are hurting today, so I think I'll take a break. You should hurry along home," Tsumugi said brusquely before disappearing into her bedroom, her hunched frame looking more frail than usual.

"Now listen, Yomo, what the heck are—"

But Yomo was already gone, having apparently finished what he'd come to do, leaving Asa and Uta alone together.

"Uta..."

Uta offered a quiet smile. "Wanna head home?"

Asa was more dejected than she'd expected at not getting the answers she wanted, her shoulders slumping.

"Well," Uta added instead, "maybe Tsumugi will want to talk with you."

"With me?"

"Yeah."

It certainly didn't appear that way. Asa turned to look back at the bedroom to which Tsumugi had slunk away.

That night, still inside the house, Asa continued to work with sidelong glances at the embroidery Tsumugi had given her. Her stitching had been rough when she'd first come here, but now it was clean and straight.

However, despite the quiet of nighttime being ideal for making progress, Asa's concentration would readily falter, and each time it did she stared off at Tsumugi's bedroom.

V

Asa woke the next day just past noon, having fallen asleep at some point, to find Uta and Tsumugi next to her. She sat up with a start.

"Ah, you're awake," Tsumugi said, as if nothing were out of the ordinary.

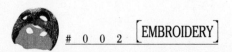 # 0 0 2 [EMBROIDERY]

"Urgh . . ." Asa nodded, feeling slightly off-kilter.

"We're going out. Get yourself ready," the old woman told her.

"Huh? Isn't it kinda early to go shopping?"

"We're going a bit farther today."

"Farther?" Asa asked, tilting her head.

Tsumugi nodded. "Yes," she replied. "We're going to see an old friend of mine."

They wound up taking the subway, eventually arriving at a hospital in the 8th Ward. Yomo's words from the night before crept back into Asa's mind. Yujiro Utsumi. He'd been hospitalized in an 8th Ward facility.

As the approached the automatic doors to the hospital, Uta stopped and said, "I'll wait here. I kind of stand out."

Asa was flustered. "Should I wait here with you, then?" She didn't stand out as much as Uta did, but she still stood out.

"No, you come with me. Just remember to hide your face," Tsumugi said.

Asa pulled her hood up and headed into the hospital.

Tsumugi led her to one of the patient rooms. "Here," she said. A nameplate reading Yujiro Utsumi hung by the door. Inside, a man somewhere around his seventies was sleeping. There were intravenous tubes and various other pieces of medical equipment connected to his body. The sight brought a quietly pained expression to Tsumugi's face, the likes of which Asa hadn't seen before.

"Old lady, is this guy . . .?"

"Yes. He's my former lover. And the man who commissioned the mask in that photo."

"Huh? Wait, so is this guy a Ghoul?" But Asa had never heard of a Ghoul receiving human medical treatment.

"No, he's human," Tsumugi affirmed for her. "But you could perhaps consider him a Ghoul all the same."

"Huh? What do you mean?"

Tsumugi silently reached out with a wrinkled hand to touch Yujiro's face. When he showed no response, she closed her eyes tight. "He would eat people," she said.

Asa's breath caught in her throat. "A . . . a human who . . . ate other humans?"

"Yes. You could call him a connoisseur of human flesh, I suppose. And he raised Ghouls to help him indulge in his desires."

At each and every turn, this story was getting harder to comprehend. Asa listened, perplexed, as Tsumugi went on. "He would have them kidnap young women and then butcher them. And if his cannibalistic ways were ever discovered, his plan was to pin all the blame on the Ghouls he'd raised, and flee."

The tale was starting to make Asa's head hurt as she attempted to follow along, but then she suddenly remembered the mask. "So then you made that mask for one of the Ghouls this guy was raising?"

Tsumugi nodded to affirm. "I fell in love with his unconventional, bold demeanor, and so I helped him without telling another soul. However, one of his Ghouls was killed by a Ghoul investigator, and so it seems that the existence of the mask got out."

That's why the detective had that photo, Asa now realized.

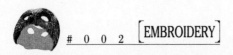 # 0 0 2 [EMBROIDERY]

"I think he realized he couldn't keep it up for long, that he'd be discovered one day, and now he wants to leave this world behind without ever being judged for his crimes."

The form of Yujiro Utsumi lay unconscious. Even Asa could tell that he would very likely die before he ever woke up again.

Tsumugi took her hand away from Yujiro's cheek and murmured, "But judgment is deserved."

The sun had already set by the time they made it back to the 20th Ward, and the surroundings were dark. Uta had already parted ways with them, leaving Asa and Tsumugi to walk alone.

"About what we discussed today," Tsumugi said as her house was just coming into view. "I'll leave it to your judgment whether you tell anyone about it or not."

She must have meant the stuff about Yujiro. "I'm not really the kinda person to spread rumors."

"I'm not worried about that sort of thing."

For some reason, those words made Asa stop as if she'd been rooted in place, and she gazed at Tsumugi from behind. The old woman was so small. Just what was it she wanted from Asa?

At that moment, however, Asa felt an unsettling breeze run through the air.

"Huh?!" Asa sensed a sudden presence descending from above. On reflex, she looked up to see insectoid wings spread wide. Next

she saw a man's silhouette, followed by a mask.

The mask looked similar to the one Tsumugi had made at Yujiro's request, but at the moment that didn't matter. The man's wings—his ukaku—stirred the air.

"Old lady, look out!"

A hail of projectiles rained down on them. Asa reached out for Tsumugi, who was walking ahead of her. However, the projectiles from the ukaku pierced through Asa's outstretched hand, and then her body.

She cried out in pain, and as she was about to hit the concrete, she saw Tsumugi take an even more grievous injury and then collapse.

"Old lady!" Asa cried out, pushing off the ground with her injured right hand and hurrying over to Tsumugi. The masked Ghoul who'd attacked them blocked her way, however.

"Damn you!" Asa ground her molars together hard. She called on her power to release itself, splitting her skin as it rose to the surface in the scaled pattern of her rinkaku. "You son of a bitch!" She turned about and attempted to strike the masked Ghoul with all her might, but he leapt nimbly aside to dodge. It figured that he was capable. Now she had no choice but to focus her mind wholly on killing him.

"Ngh . . ."

Asa's eyes darted over to Tsumugi's silhouette. The pool of blood was growing ever larger. Asa's mind raced, her thought process becoming muddled.

"Not paying attention?" There was no time to react. The man

closed the distance all at once and attacked Asa from close range.

"Argh!" The kick caught Asa hard in the abdomen, sending her hurtling back into a telephone pole. The man then kicked her in the face where she huddled, and proceeded to stomp on her fallen form.

"Who the hell are you? Why are you wearing the old lady's mask?" Asa asked, catching sight of the embroidered mask. Wasn't the Ghoul who'd had Tsumugi's mask supposed to be dead?

"You have no idea what's going on with us, huh? Meh, whatever. Losing our breadwinner's made us a bit cranky. So I guess I'll just torture you to death, and—"

The man stopped short and backed away from Asa. She couldn't understand why, but then, across the street, she saw a figure emerge from the shadows.

"I'd appreciate it if you stopped that."

Asa could hardly believe it. "Uta?" But he'd already gone off.

"Uta, from the 4th Ward, huh? Hmph. This doesn't look good . . ." The man looked over at Tsumugi as he backed away from his intimidating foe. The old woman wasn't moving at all. "Well, guess I accomplished what I came to do. No point in sticking around. See ya!" The man then leapt into the air and darted off.

Ordinarily, Asa would have given chase, but now wasn't the time for that. "Old lady!" She rushed to Tsumugi's side. She had injuries all over, and was bleeding out. Asa tried using both hands to stanch the bleeding, but all she succeeded in doing was getting them soaked red. Her own Ghoul body had already begun to recover, whereas Tsumugi's life was draining away.

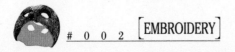 # 0 0 2 [EMBROIDERY]

"Th-that's right! The hospital!" If she took Tsumugi there, they could help her.

As Asa was about to lift Tsumugi, the old woman managed to croak out some words. "You fool. I told you . . ."

"Old lady!"

"How do you plan on explaining this? With all these strange punctures . . . the doctors will realize . . . I've been attacked by a Ghoul . . . "

"So what? You *have* been attacked by a Ghoul!"

"And then the Ghoul investigators will come. If they investigate me . . . they'll find out about you. Worst case, you might be killed . . ." With that, Tsumugi coughed, a large amount of blood spilling from her mouth.

Asa had killed countless people, had seen blood so many times before, but the sight of Tsumugi's blood now made her tremble in fear.

"You can't save me . . . I'd hoped for things to end this way."

"You . . . you *wanted* this?"

Tsumugi's eyes narrowed, and she stared up at the nighttime sky. "Yujiro raised two Ghouls . . . one who did the kidnapping, the other who did the butchering. The one who died was the kidnapper, so the one just now must've been the butcher . . ."

"There were two of them? But wait, why did you want this?" Asa couldn't make sense of any of it.

Tsumugi went on, her voice halting. "He was long afraid that I might expose everything. He behaved while Yujiro was around, but now that Yujiro's not long for this world . . . I suppose he decided to take action."

It was visibly painful for her to talk, her upper body heaving with each raspy breath. The sight of her suffering like this brought a pain to Asa's chest. "Why didn't you say something before? I could have done something! This didn't have to happen to you!"

Asa's shouting made Tsumugi narrow her eyes again. "I just wanted to take responsibility for the life I've led."

"Old lady . . ."

"This is fine . . ."

In the hospital room, Tsumugi had murmured something about deserving judgment. It seemed she hadn't been referring only to Yujiro, but to herself as well.

Her eyes grew heavier, her pupils disappearing behind her eyelids. She was dying, about to drift off into the dark. It hadn't been a long time, but the days she'd spent with Tsumugi flashed through Asa's memories.

"No," she said, feeling a heat growing in her chest. "Don't you die on me, old lady! I've had so much fun . . . I've had so much fun spending time with you!" She was a human, and an elderly woman, at that. She would have been completely beneath the old Asa's notice; now the girl was despairing so much that she found it hard to breathe. "Your masks were so amazing, and your embroidery is amazing too! I mean you were a pain in the ass at first, but at some point, I . . . I started having fun, and . . ."

Tears fell from Asa's eyes, one after the other.

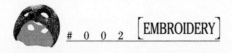 # 0 0 2 〔EMBROIDERY〕

"There was a warmth inside me, and sometimes even a tightness in my chest . . . and right now it just hurts so much . . . Don't die, old lady . . . You can't. You still have so much more to teach me!"

Uta silently cast his gaze aside as Asa shouted. There was a sudden warm sensation on her cheek. She watched as Tsumugi took the palm of her hand and roughly wiped away the tears.

"You're getting all sentimental on me," the old woman said, tears streaming from her own eyes. "Don't do shoddy work now, Asa," she added with a tiny smile, her wrinkled face wrinkling up all the more.

With that, her hand limply fell away.

"Old lady?" Asa looked at Tsumugi in disbelief. But she wasn't moving anymore. She wasn't answering. "Old lady!"

Asa drew the body up into her arms and held it close, unable to hold back her scream. *"Tsumugi!"*

"Uta, did you know all this from the beginning?"

They were back at Tsumugi's house. Asa had washed the blood away and lain her out atop the bed. She looked into the dead woman's face, her voice dry. "That someone was after her, I mean. And if I'd known, would there . . . could I have protected her?"

Uta shook his head. He looked back and forth between Asa and Tsumugi, and then calmly muttered, "All I wanted was to take a look at Tsumugi's embroidery. And . . ."

"And what?"

"And I thought you two would have really good chemistry, so . . ."

Asa looked back at Uta.

"I wanted you two to meet each other."

Asa's eyes went wide. Then she bit her lip hard as she looked at him.

Even though the loss hurt, even though there was sadness in death, even though Tsumugi was a human and Asa was a Ghoul . . .

. . . she was glad to have met her.

She truly felt that, deep down.

VI

Several days after Tsumugi's passing, Asa stood outside the 8th Ward police station in the full glow of the streetlights. A man stepped out of the station and came over to her.

0 0 2 [EMBROIDERY]

"Sorry I haven't been in touch. Did you happen to find who made that mask?" It was the detective, Morimine. Asa had been in contact with him.

"I didn't, no. I asked around, but none of my contacts had any hunches to go on," she lied blithely.

"I see. Well, I mean, thanks for taking the trouble to look into this for me. I appreciate your cooperation." Morimine was at least quick to thank her for the effort. He was probably a decent guy. Which meant he might do what humans would call "the right thing."

"I do have some other information, though."

"Other information?"

Asa nodded. "Promise not to ask too many questions?" she asked.

Morimine regarded the serious look in her eyes, and steeled his resolve. "Sure."

"You're working on the Yujiro Utsumi case, is that right, detective?"

Shock spread out across Morimine's face. He was about to ask something, but closed his mouth, swallowed, and gave a simple, "Yes."

Asa continued. "Apparently, Yujiro Utsumi used Ghouls to abduct young women, and then he ate their flesh." She shouldn't get this involved with human affairs, and there was no guarantee that she wouldn't hang for the decision at some later point. But Asa was willing to take the risk.

"You're saying that Yujiro Utsumi ate human flesh despite

being a human himself?" Morimine asked in disbelief, rubbing at his forehead.

"I don't have any proof, so whether you believe me or not is up to you, detective."

Asa was surprised at how quick Morimine was to respond. "No, I believe you," he said. "Thanks to you, all the pieces have come together. Guess this maybe was a human's doing after all." Then, something else appeared to click inside his head. "In that case, then Otokaze might . . . Oh, this is bad. I've got to stop her!"

Morimine turned on his heel, clearly unable to hold back his racing thoughts, but stopped long enough to look back and say, "Thank you so much for all your assistance."

"Is it cool to just leave me be when I know this secret?" Asa asked.

The corner of Morimine's mouth curled up slightly at Asa's inordinate forthrightness. "You've changed your face," he said.

"Huh?"

"A bunch of stuff happened to me a little while back, so I get it. It's a good look for you," Morimine said. Then, he offered a casual "See ya!" before heading off.

Left by herself, Asa reached up to stroke her cheek. "What's that about?" she muttered quietly to herself. "Well, I guess it's to be expected."

The day Tsumugi died, Uta had told her, *"Tsumugi said she wanted to leave this house to you. And she told me to list you as one of her family members. I'll see about having Itori handle the relevant*

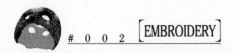 # 0 0 2 [EMBROIDERY]

paperwork for that."

"She wanted me to have the house?"

"Way back when, this used to be Tsumugi's dressmaking shop. She said she wanted it turned back into a shop, whether it's a mask shop or whatever else."

She didn't have the skill to open a shop. But someday, once she'd gotten better, she would open one there. She couldn't do shoddy work.

Wound around her arm now was the scarf Tsumugi had embroidered. She clutched it tightly and turned her gaze back ahead. "All right, let's go home!"

Back home, where some trace of Tsumugi still lingered.

東京 —— [VOID] —— 喰種 ——

[PHOTOGRAPHY]

*T*he tiny archivist reveals the truth through snippets cut from the flow of time.

"Idol Fest?" Chie Hori repeated, curious. It was eleven o'clock at night, and the crowds around the 20th Ward station were beginning to thin out.

"Yeah, tomorrow in the 1st Ward, apparently," affirmed the familiar street musician.

Chie stroked the camera that hung from her neck as she murmured the words to herself one more time. "Idol Fest, huh?" She had close-cropped black hair and bright, round eyes that darted this way and that in no real hurry. By outward appearances she looked like a grade-schooler, though in fact she was a grown young woman attending university. She devoted far more time to her hobby than her schooling, however, and rarely even went to campus.

That hobby, as the camera that hung around her neck made clear, was photography. She'd long had a love for taking pictures, the thought of it occupying her every waking hour. While her height never increased, her fervor for photography did, and now she scurried about to and fro in search of interesting pictures to take.

She'd returned to the 20th Ward several days ago, but here and there she still asked her acquaintances if there was anything interesting going on when she ran into them.

"Abrupt as ever, Chiehori," the musician laughed as he resituated the guitar that hung over his shoulder. "I hear some big-name idols have been invited. I'm going too!"

"You're an idol singer now, Ikuma?"

"Oh, no, no! I'm just going to help load stuff." His name was Ikuma Momochi, an affable young man who'd moved to Tokyo at age twenty to follow his musical aspirations. By day he worked for a shipping company, and by night he took his trusty guitar out by the train station to sing. "Apparently it's an all-female idol event. But you don't strike me as having much interest in idol singers."

He then handed Chie a piece of candy he'd received from a fan. Though he'd gotten used to life in Tokyo, he still had his old accent, along with a big secret.

"It's too bad you can't eat candy," Chie said.

"It's too bad I can't eat *any* human food." While Ikuma appeared to be a typical young man in pursuit of his dreams, he was, in reality, a Ghoul. The only thing he was able to eat was human flesh, and his

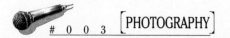

0 0 3 [PHOTOGRAPHY]

eyes would go awash with red when he was on the cusp of danger.

But although he was a Ghoul, he was a more gentle sort, one who tried his utmost to live as a part of human society. Evidently, he didn't kill people, and fed only on the flesh of suicides.

"So anyhow, how's Tsukiyama doing?" Ikuma said, asking about one of his fellow Ghouls.

"Tsukiyama? He's out being a stalker right now."

"Man, Tsukiyama's got this weird ability that, no matter what he does, it just comes across as such a 'Tsukiyama' thing to do, y'know?"

And Tsukiyama didn't do things at all like Ikuma did. No, Shu Tsukiyama was a belligerent Ghoul, and no means were too craven for him to obtain the fine meals he constantly sought. As someone who enjoyed the act of hunting, he was certainly a very "ghoulish" Ghoul from a human perspective, but his very particular tastes evidently made him something of an oddball maverick even to his own kind.

Tsukiyama and Chie Hori had been inseparable since high school, ever since Chie managed to snap a photo of him feeding. Her nose for a good scoop had led her to follow her classmate in secret, and she'd gotten the picture she'd been after.

At first Tsukiyama had wanted to kill Chie for taking his picture, but his interest in her seemed to grow upon seeing her unflinchingly taking photos of whatever situation she encountered. Since then they'd been close associates, despite the lack of desire to actually interact.

And lately, Tsukiyama had been absorbed by thoughts of his

current prey.

"He says he's found some super tasty-looking prey, but there's some trouble in actually getting to eat it."

"Huh. Sounds like someone's in a bit of a bind."

Chie popped the candy she'd gotten from Ikuma into her mouth. "Mm-hmm," she agreed. "But more importantly, you said this Idol Fest is tomorrow, right?"

"Oh. Yeah. Wait, are you going?" He didn't think Chie would have any interest in an idol festival.

The look on Ikuma's face told Chie that there could be some rare sights, and so she pointed to her camera. "I just have a feeling I'll be able to take some neat photos!"

Ikuma's cheeks pulled back at that. "I'm a little scared by anything you'd consider 'neat,' Chie Hori."

II

It was the day of the Idol Fest that Ikuma had mentioned, and the concert grounds were brimming with an unusual enthusiasm. Stalls offering pop star merchandise lined the open plaza, and throngs of spectators were crammed together in front of the outdoor stage.

"Ohhh, I can't see a thing!" Chie had come all this way hoping to get a look at some idols, but a tall, thick wall of men blocked her view, and given her diminutive stature she had no hope of seeing over it. Taking photos from this vantage would be even

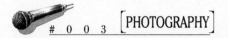

more of a problem.

"Hmmm..." Chie scanned the grounds. "Aha!" she said upon spotting a large tree far off to one side. She circled the tree in order to scope it out first, then got up on one of the roots and proceeded to climb up using footholds in the bark. Soon she reached a large branch and sat herself down on it, finally able to peek through her camera.

By zooming in, she was able to get a look at the showily dressed idol singers dancing about. There was a surprising assortment of them, some clad in adorable pastel-colored outfits, others scurrying about like they were in some comedy routine, and everything in between. "Ah, so this is what sort of event this is," Chie said, whimsically clicking the shutter on her camera.

While she was checking the photos she'd taken, the cheers of the crowd started to die down. It looked as though a minor idol singer, one who didn't look like they'd be on television, was performing on center stage.

"Huh?" Chie muttered as another meek-looking girl got up on stage.

"Next up, we have college student idol singer Mitsuba!"

Chie readied her camera again. *So, even girls like this do idol singing?* The music began to play as the introduction finished, and the girl called Mitsuba started to sing.

"Oh wow," Chie murmured. The girl wore a frilled skirt and a hair band with ribbons. She certainly looked the part of an idol singer, and her voice carried clear and distinct, but here and there her

expression looked sad and lonely, contrary to her cheerful tune.

The time she'd been allotted was short, and before long her song came to an end. Upon finishing, she bowed her head and then hurried backstage and out of sight. Then, a sudden voice jolted Chie. "Hey, you! It's not safe to climb up there!"

It was one of the venue's security guards, shouting at Chie up in the tree. Chie slid back down, and then made her way back over toward the stage.

"H-hey!" called the security guard, presumably wanting Chie to stop so he could press for more of an explanation, but she disappeared into the massive crowd near the stage. She then calmly inspected the photos on her camera.

"Whoa!" It was a photo of Mitsuba, who'd just been performing. Despite her flashy title of idol singer, her expression was flat, her eyes vacant. Her lips were faintly parted as if to call out to someone, sadness about to issue forth from them.

"Now just *what* is the story here, I wonder?"

Slipping her way out of the Idol Fest, Chie made her way to a nearby café and transferred her data to the laptop she carried in her backpack. She sipped hot cocoa topped with a dollop of fresh cream as she reviewed her photos on the larger monitor—specifically, the ones she'd taken of Mitsuba.

According to what Chie could find on the Internet, the girl was nineteen years old. She had a somber disposition and wasn't very self-assertive, to the point where even her fans seemed perplexed as to why she'd become an idol singer.

Well, that's certainly begging for a follow-up, Chie thought to herself as she went on to check the other photographs she'd taken that day.

The bell at the café entrance jangled as a new customer came in, and on some curious instinct, Chie looked up.

"Aha." Her hunch had been right: slipping in through the door was none other than the Ghoul gourmet, Shu Tsukiyama.

He took notice of Chie soon enough himself. *"Oddio!"* he cried out, his right hand extended, his left set against his forehead as he arched his body slightly. At once, all eyes were upon him. Could

he just not stand *not* being the center of attention? The fact that he could lead such an active life without being caught by the CCG made Chie think that, while the CCG might be made up of professionals, they certainly weren't perfect.

"Oh, Hori! Have you been lying in ambush for me?"

"No, it's nothing like that."

Tsukiyama sat down across from Chie as if it were

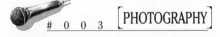

0 0 3 [PHOTOGRAPHY]

a matter of course. "Then what have you been doing?" he asked.

"Organizing photos."

"Ha ha! Ever the shutterbug! C'mon, show me what you've got, my little insect!" Tsukiyama said, gracefully extending his hand, palm up.

Chie plopped the laptop into his outstretched hand, which promptly smacked down onto the table, Tsukiyama having seemingly underestimated how heavy it would be. "God, and you're still such a tomboy, too," he said, his expression unflinching, the computer still atop his palm, clicking away at the keys with his free hand like it was a piano. "You've been taking pictures of some pretty fancy stuff, haven't you?" He seemed surprised that Chie would have taken pictures of trendy pop singers. His eyes were fixed on the screen as his fingers methodically tabbed from one photo to the next.

When he got to one photo, however, his fingers stopped. "Hmm..."

It was a photo of Mitsuba.

"White lines down to her throat like a Greek sculpture, her eyes like a cocktail of sadness... Well now, isn't she quite a marvelous subject to be photographed!"

"They said her name's Mitsuba," Chie said, eyeing the photo as she took the laptop back from Tsukiyama. "I feel like I could take a much better picture of her than this!"

Tsukiyama let out a nasal hum, sipping at the coffee one of the employees brought him. "By the way, Hori, I've got a real obsession right now."

"It's Kaneki, isn't it?"

Ken Kaneki, a Ghoul from the 20th Ward who apparently worked part time at the café Anteiku. Tsukiyama had followed him around previously with the hopes of eating him, but had since come to work together with him. His other companions weren't quite as trusting, and seemed to exclude him, but Tsukiyama wasn't the sort to be down about that.

"Ah, so the tale that Kaneki and I weave has indeed reached your ears!" Tsukiyama said, raising his right hand high. "Ever since we began working together, every day is spicier and spicier! You can tell, can't you? That I have this glow I never possessed before!"

"I'm sure Kaneki's wallet is happy with that, at any rate."

"*Non*. Riches are just another form of power. Which is a price worth paying for Kaneki's time! It's the ample time we *do* spend together that so deepens our trusting relationship."

"You sound like some old man talking about his favorite hostess," Chie said. Was he of a mind to one day betray that trust with a sword, only to lick at blood that dripped down from the blade? *No*, Chie thought blithely. She didn't think anyone would trust him in his whole life.

"Oh, speaking of which," Chie said, suddenly remembering something, "what are you doing for 'food' nowadays?" Apparently, Kaneki was scouring the wards in search of something. If that was the case, then Tsukiyama was probably going along with him, and considering that Tsukiyama's finicky, particular tastes currently had him craving Kaneki above anything else, Chie had to wonder what

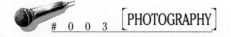

0 0 3 [PHOTOGRAPHY]

he'd been eating instead.

"I'm getting by," Tsukiyama replied quickly enough. "After having set eyes on Kaneki, everything else looks like such meager fare—*that* is how exquisite Kaneki is!"

Tsukiyama looked like he was ready to launch into another spiel about Kaneki when Chie blurted out, "Wait, what? The self-styled 'gourmet' has been getting by on *junk food*?" Her eyes were wide with astonishment.

Tsukiyama stared back at her, the look on his face making it look as if he'd just been struck by lightning. "I *do* beg your pardon?"

"I know you've had your sights set on Kaneki, and you've also never been one to skimp when it comes to meals. I guess people really *do* change." Well, Tsukiyama wasn't necessarily a "person," per se.

Chie put her computer back into her backpack and stood up. She tried to leave Tsukiyama with the check, but he held out his right arm to block her path. "Hold it right there!" His brow was furrowed, and he had an almost exaggerated look of pain on his face as he forced out his words. "Oh, Hori! Your words pierce my delicate heart, sweet and smooth, like a knife through cheesecake!"

"But you've never even eaten a cheesecake."

Ignoring Chie's words, Tsukiyama continued repentantly. "Oh, Hori, it's just like you said. I, Shu Tsukiyama, born to seek out and consume only the finest cuisine, have had to stoop so low as to consume common food. And once I know what Kaneki tastes like, nothing else will ever be worth tasting again! However"—he suddenly thrust a finger at Chie—"I have decided that, though she might not meet the standards of my discerning palate, I must have this delicious, despairing diva you've shown me!"

"Huh?" That finally got a reaction out of Chie. Here was Tsukiyama, talking about how he wanted to eat Mitsuba. "No way. I need to take pictures of her."

"Seeing that picture finally stirred my appetite after so long! Not as much as Kaneki, of course, but there's something in her that makes her such an enticing cocktail. I am sorry, but she *will* be mine."

Tsukiyama's proud laugh pushed Chie over the edge, and without a word she took what was left of the syrupy cocoa and dumped it over his head as hard as she could before marching out of the café.

"H-Hori! Do you have *any* idea how long it takes to do my hair right?!"

Now Tsukiyama would probably go home and take a shower. Chie adjusted the backpack bouncing against her back, got out her smartphone, and began a web search on Mitsuba. She needed to make sure she found her before Tsukiyama did.

III

"Guess this is the place," Chie said, looking up at the apartment building. Having heard that Mitsuba lived in housing provided by her agency, Chie had been able to deduce her address from photos and statements she'd posted to her blog, along with other eyewitness accounts from the Internet.

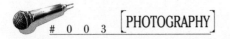

It was already past midnight, and given the possibility that Tsu-kiyama might well use his wealth to gather information, Chie figured there was a fifty-fifty chance the girl was still safe.

"Well, the lights in her room are still on." Chie made her way up to the second-floor apartment and rang the doorbell.

"Yes?" came a reply from inside. "Who is it?" Chie recognized Mitsuba's voice from the Idol Fest. It seemed she was safe after all—but still, it wouldn't be too surprising for Tsukiyama to turn up at any time.

Chie faced the peephole and said, "I've come to deliver some photographs."

"Photographs?" She was bound to be confused by that, but she also didn't seem to be terribly wary of someone who looked like a grade-schooler, and so she opened the door, visibly curious. "Who asked you to deliver these photographs, miss?"

In a complete change of pace from her outfit at the Idol Fest, Mitsuba was dressed far more casually in jeans and a three-quarter shirt. Probably nobody would suspect she was an idol singer if they saw her out on the street wearing that, but now wasn't the time to dwell on that sort of thing.

"Pardon the interruption," Chie said, slipping her way in through the open door without bothering to ask permission. Once inside, she took the intense perfume she'd brought out of her backpack and sprayed its scent around the room.

"Whoa, what?!" Mitsuba cried out, eyes going wide with bewilderment. Chie headed farther inside and started spraying with another type of perfume. "Um, miss? What are you doing?"

The different scents intermingled, stirring up a stench that almost made it difficult to breathe inside the one-room apartment. Tsukiyama ought to find the vulgar scent repugnant, to the point where being awash in it would be more than he could stand, making him unable to do much of anything without first taking a break for a shower.

Chie scanned the room, ignoring the confused Mitsuba behind her, who clearly wasn't sure how to deal with this. "Huh?" the girl squeaked out as Chie unlatched the window, then picked up the cell phone and wallet that were on the table and tossed them to her. Flustered, Mitsuba managed to catch them.

"Okay, now let's go and—" Chie began, stopping as she noticed the picture hanging by the front door. It was a family photo showing a young Mitsuba, her parents, and a girl Chie guessed was Mitsuba's older sister. Chie picked up the photograph, forcibly handed it off, then said, "Okay!" as she grabbed hold of Mitsuba's arm and dragged her outside.

"Miss, I, ah . . . I don't know what this is all about, but . . ." Mitsuba was quite flustered, but Chie could feel something in the air behind them, like little pinpricks, and she shushed the girl before hiding behind a telephone pole. Watching Mitsuba's apartment from the shadows, Chie could see someone trying to sneak in through the window.

"Hey, what's . . ." Mitsuba had noticed the suspicious man now as well. He opened the window, slipped fluidly inside, and then, a

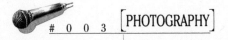

0 0 3 [PHOTOGRAPHY]

mere moment later, jumped right back out, holding his nose.

"Guess we can call the scent bomb a huge success," Chie said. She walked quietly so as not to catch Tsukiyama's attention, then broke into a run after rounding the corner at an intersection.

"M-miss, what's going on? Who *is* that man?"

"I have a name, you know. It's Chie Hori," Chie said, introducing herself.

"Chie Hori?"

"Yeah."

By now they'd come out onto a main thoroughfare. Chie stuck out her right hand and hailed a taxi. "Come on, get in."

"Wait, hold on. Where are we going?"

Chie felt it was only fair to give poor, perplexed young girl another hint. "Mitsuba, you're being hunted by a Ghoul."

Mitsuba stiffened visibly.

"Come with me if you want to live."

———————————

"Where are we?" Mitsuba asked as they got out of the taxi, fearfully inspecting her surroundings.

"We're near a Ghoul detention center." Up ahead, the building was visible, encircled by a tall fence. There was no telling what might be inside.

"Then we're in the 23rd Ward?"

"You know it, then?"

"Yes. I used to live in the 23rd Ward a while back, so I've heard of it. But wait, wasn't there a breakout at this detention facility a few months ago?"

She was right. Several months earlier, a number of Ghouls had indeed managed to escape from the Ghoul detention center, and the 23rd Ward had been in a state of high alert ever since as a result. "Yep. According to the rumors, some of the Ghoul escapees were particularly nasty, too," Chie said.

"But Miss Hori, hold on. Doesn't that mean it's dangerous around here?" Mitsuba seemed like she thought one of these nasty Ghouls could be right next to her, and she continued to uneasily inspect her surroundings.

"Don't worry, we'll be fine. After the breakout, a whole bunch of Ghoul investigators were assigned to the 23rd Ward, and Cochlea had its security beefed up a ton," Chie said as she led them to a nearby park. With a soft huff, she sat down on a bench and patted the spot beside her, which Mitsuba promptly took.

"So what do you mean, I'm being hunted by a Ghoul?" she asked.

A picture being worth a thousand words, Chie took her laptop out of her backpack and showed her the photo she'd taken of Tsu-kiyama feeding from way back when. A tiny squeak of fear escaped Mitsuba's throat, and she went pale.

"Apparently this Ghoul has taken a liking to you, Mitsuba, and he's decided to track you down. Which, uh, might be partially my fault."

"*Your* fault, Miss Hori?"

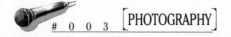 # 0 0 3 [PHOTOGRAPHY]

"Yeah. This Ghoul's an acquaintance of mine. His name's Tsukiyama."

"You've got a Ghoul for an acquaintance? Then . . . then does that mean you're . . ."

Probably she was wondering whether Chie was also a Ghoul like Tsukiyama. Under the circumstances, it may have been reasonable to think.

"Hey, I might have a Ghoul acquaintance, but I'm very human!" Chie said promptly, to clear things up.

"But sheltering a Ghoul isn't something you . . ."

"Sheltering? Hey, I'm just leaving him be," Chie replied, pulling up the photo that started this whole mess. "I wound up showing him this picture of you singing at the Idol Fest, and that sparked his interest."

Mitsuba gasped as she saw the picture. "Is . . . that what I look like when I sing?" It was as if she'd been shown a picture of someone she didn't recognize. She just stared at it, dumbstruck. After a moment, however, she snapped out of it. "You're a very talented photographer, Miss Hori," she said.

Chie slipped her computer back into her backpack and hopped off of the bench. "If Tsukiyama finds you, you're going to get eaten, so for starters you should probably hide for the time being. I know someone who has a place here in the 23rd Ward, so let's see about hiding you there for a while."

"But Miss Hori, since this is a Ghoul matter, shouldn't we take this to the CCG? They should be able to help me, right?" Mitsuba asked.

"That's a no-go," Chie replied. "The CCG could harbor you for a while, sure, but it's not like you can just live there forever, right? And investigators can't guard you 24/7, either—and besides, Tsukiyama's likely stronger than they'd be, anyway."

Chie went on. "Also, assuming we did somehow eliminate Tsukiyama, his Ghoul family would be out for revenge, and you'd wind up being killed anyway. They're kind of a . . . unique bunch."

"Then it sounds like there's no way to save me . . ." It was understandable for Mitsuba to lose hope. Even just having Tsukiyama after her was frightening enough.

But Chie hadn't come to her without a plan.

"I don't know if we can pull it off, but I have an idea of how to avoid him for the time being." A glimmer of hope appeared on Mitsuba's face. "I feel like I could take much better pictures of you, Mitsuba." Which was why Chie couldn't let her get eaten by Tsukiyama.

Mitsuba probably didn't even understand half of what Chie meant, but she seemed to have at least some idea. Standing up from the bench, she lowered her head. "If you would, please."

———————

Chie took Mitsuba to a high-end condominium not too far from the Ghoul detention center.

"This is incredible . . ." the girl said as she took in the sights of the extravagant interior design and dazzling decorations. The window offered a great look out at the nighttime cityscape.

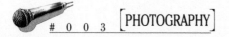 # 0 0 3 [PHOTOGRAPHY]

"Let's hide out here for now. Oh, and you should probably contact the people from your agency. Let them know you probably won't be back for a while."

"Oh. Yes, right . . ."

Chie sat down on the floor in a position she was quite used to, then got her computer out of her backpack and booted it up. She then got out some snacks, rolled up her sleeves, and opened her photo files.

"What are you doing, Miss Hori?"

"Mmm . . . just picking out some pictures."

"Picking them out for what?"

"Figure I might be able to sell some." It was too much to hope that she'd be able to win out over Tsukiyama on her lonesome. If she could sell some of her photos, she'd be able to purchase some assistance.

"Oh, by the way," Chie said then, remembering the photo of Mitsuba's family amidst trying to figure out the next stages of her plan, "what's your family like, Mitsuba?" Knowing Tsukiyama, there was a chance he'd make contact with her family in order to get information. That wouldn't be too bad by itself, but it would be a disaster if Chie blurted out that Tsukiyama's particular sensibilities might get the better of him and cause him to eat her family as part of some taste-comparison test. "It just might be a little risky if Tsukiyama makes contact with them."

Mitsuba's eyes drooped at that. "You don't need to worry about that," she murmured. "My father remarried and is living overseas now. I get email from him sometimes, but that's it, so he knows almost nothing about what's going on with me."

She set the family photo atop the table and clutched her knees. Tsukiyama could probably still get to someone overseas if he caught wind of things, but given his current obsession with Kaneki, Chie doubted he'd go through the effort. So Mistuba's father was probably safe.

"What about the other two?" Chie asked, looking at the photo set on the table.

Mitsuba huddled herself up even tighter. "They're . . . missing."

Chie stopped her typing and looked up. "Both of them?

"Did they go missing together?"

"No, separately," Mistuba said. "Sorry. I'm not really explaining it right, huh?" she added with a bitter laugh.

Chie shook her head. "It's all right," she said. "Would you mind telling me about them?"

For a while, Mitsuba was lost in thought, but then seemed to find the resolve to talk. "My sister ran away when she was in high school. My mother was worried sick over it, and a year later she went missing too."

Mitsuba's sister was about ten years older than her, and had longed to become an idol singer since she was little. Back at home, she was always dressing up in cute little outfits and singing with a toy

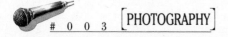
0 0 3 [PHOTOGRAPHY]

microphone. Her mother and father would laugh and smile as they watched her, praising her singing.

As her sister grew up, however, her mother began to frown upon these antics. *"You're in high school now! How long are you going to cling to this silly dream of becoming an idol singer?"*

"It's not some silly dream! I'm serious about this!"

Mitsuba's sister held off on taking her college entrance exams, and almost every day she and her mother had arguments about her future. Her sister said that she wanted to quit school and go into the entertainment industry, but her mother staunchly forbade it. Her father stayed out of it, pretending not to notice as the other two argued incessantly. Mitsuba had wanted to support her sister, but her mother's threatening, oppressive demeanor forced her into silence.

The arguments came to a head when Mitsuba's sister went and got herself business cards from an entertainment agency.

It had been a summer day, the air filled with the droning of cicadas. There was the usual angry shouting from Mitsuba's mother and shrill cries from her sister. At some point, Mitsuba's mother raised her hand and struck her daughter across the cheek.

"Mommy, stop it!" Mitsuba hurriedly interposed herself between them after seeing her sister fall to the floor. Her sister shoved her out of the way, however, and got back up, a hand pressed to where she'd been hit on the cheek.

"You used to encourage me so much when I was little! You're such a bitch, mom!" her sister spat before gathering up her things and rushing out the front door, slamming it closed behind her.

"Sis . . ."

"Leave her!" Mitsuba's mother snapped before she could chase after her sister, then stomped off to the kitchen, indignant. This wasn't the first time her sister had stormed off, and so Mitsuba was sure she'd come back home before long. Previously, it had turned out that she'd actually just gone to her voice lessons.

But that time, when her sister left the house in tears after her mother hit her, was the last time Mitsuba ever saw her. She never came back.

After that, her mother and father began arguing daily. Her father would tell his wife it was her fault. Despite having gone for so long watching their fights and ignoring them, he still had the gall to blame her every day for their daughter never coming home.

Her mother would cry, tears falling onto the photo of her daughter she clutched in her hands day in and day out.

And then, a year after Mitsuba's sister disappeared, her mother vanished as well, leaving only a note that read: *"I'm sorry."*

"Ah, maybe that's it," Chie said, feeling like she'd hit upon the answer now that Mitsuba's explanation was finished. "The sad look on your face, I mean." She brought up the photo on her computer screen again.

"I thought that if I went into the entertainment industry, I might find my sister. Given how badly she'd wanted to become an idol

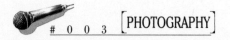

singer, I was sure that's where she'd be working. And if I got famous enough, maybe my mother would see me on TV. But now, I . . . I don't really think either of them is alive anymore . . ."

"Hmm. I see," Chie said, crossing her arms, rocking about restlessly as her eyes darted around. She then got out a pen and some paper and handed them to Mitsuba. "Write down the names of everyone in your family."

"Huh?"

"I'm gonna do some searching." Because just maybe, she might find the key to all this.

———————————

It was after three o'clock in the morning, and the exhausted Mitsuba lay on the floor. Chie worked at curating her photos while also running searches online, scanning through news reports. A run of burglaries. Hospital patients suffering injuries. Sports news. Financial data.

"Hmm?" As Chie was following this narrow thread of hers, one word unexpectedly jumped out at her. "Huh . . ."

She wanted to go and look into it right away, but she couldn't well leave Mitsuba here. Instead, she called up a helpful friend of hers.

"Hey, Ikuma? There's a little something I could use your help with . . ."

IV

"You know the 23rd Ward is terrifying, right, Chie?" Ikuma fretted. It was the next day, and he'd come bearing plastic supermarket bags in both hands. Chie had asked him to look into things, and also to pick up some food, supplies, and other daily necessities. It seemed, however, that having to set foot in the 23rd Ward while it was on special alert was something of a tribulation for a Ghoul like him. He continued to look around restlessly.

"Thanks! This is a big help," Chie said. "So what do you think?"

"Well, it looks like you might be onto something with regard to that thing you had me look into."

"Aha. I thought as much. Do you think you'd be able to get in touch with someone for me next?" Chie asked, handing Ikuma some notes she'd written down for what to do next.

The conflicted look on Ikuma's face was quite unlike anything Chie had seen from Tsukiyama. "Chie, I'm not really that good at this sort of thing. I might be a Ghoul, but I'm really just a normal guy."

"I wouldn't ask if I didn't

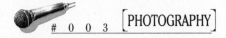

0 0 3 [PHOTOGRAPHY]

think you could pull it off."

"Sheesh, no pressure or anything. I mean, I guess I'll see what I can do," Ikuma uttered meekly. "Besides, that poor girl must have it really rough," he added. At least he seemed worried for Mitsuba. "I never should've told you about that Idol Fest . . ."

With that, Ikuma hurried away from the condominium, a distant look in his eyes. He clearly felt like he alone bore responsibility for this whole mess.

Chie had Ikuma helping her out as she spent day and night at the 23rd Ward condo gathering information. Before she knew it a week had passed, and it was dawning on her that she might well be in for a long haul here.

"Hmmm . . . This is taking a while." Chie had actually made contact with someone who could turn this whole thing around at the drop of a hat, but given her own position and not wanting to put her contact too on edge, she hadn't been able to make much forward progress.

She hadn't heard from her contact today, either, and it was already past sunset. *Well, not much I can do about it now*, Chie thought as she took her gaze away from her computer screen and began to fiddle with her camera.

"Hm?" She heard a quiet voice, singing. Straining to make it out, she recognized it as an idol song that had been popular a long while back. Mitsuba was singing, apparently. Chie headed to the back room and poked her head in to check on Mitsuba.

"I'm sorry. Was I being too loud?"

Chie shook her head. "It's all right," she said. "You have fond memories of that song?"

"My sister used to sing it a lot. Back when my mom and dad used to listen to her, smiles on their faces, and tell her how good she was." Mitsuba's eyes narrowed with visible nostalgia. "I think my sister was really happy for all that. Even after she grew up, she'd always carry around her old toy microphone in her bag . . ."

The look of reminiscence on her face then grew tinged with sadness. "I guess people need to learn to let go of the past," she laughed, trying to cover that up. "But how are you doing, Miss Hori?"

"No real progress. We might need to move to a new base of operations soon so that Tsukiyama doesn't find us," Chie said, and as she ran through a mental checklist of where their next safe house might be, the intercom chimed. She padded over to the front door and opened it.

There stood Ikuma, a rather serious look on his face. "Chie, I think I've got something," he said, quietly enough for Mitsuba not to overhear as he showed Chie a picture.

Chie took a good look at it, then nodded. "Got it. I hate to bother you, but do you mind coming inside?"

Every other time, Ikuma and Chie had done their business by the door, and he'd gone home as soon as things finished up. Mitsuba's eyes widened to see him actually come into the room. "Good evening," he said.

"Oh! Thank you so much for all you help." Mitsuba hadn't been informed that Ikuma was a Ghoul. Probably she just thought he was

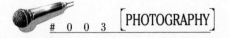

a nice, helpful young man. Today, however, she appeared to sense that something else was going on with him and Chie, and her expression stiffened.

"Mitsuba, could you come here for a sec?" Chie said, sitting down on the floor. Ikuma sat down alongside her. Mitsuba sat across from them, her eyes attentive.

Chie decided to cut straight to the point. "Mitsuba, we've tracked down your mother and your sister."

Mitsuba let out a quick, sharp gasp at the sudden news. "My . . . my mother and my sister?"

"Yes. I won't beat around the bush: your sister is already dead. Your mother stabbed someone and then attempted suicide, and is in critical condition."

"Ah . . ." That probably wasn't anything like the answer Mitsuba had been expecting. She was visibly stricken, and began to tremble as she took in Chie's words.

"Chie, did you really need to put it like that?" Ikuma said, his sympathy for Mitsuba plain.

Ignoring him, Chie kept her gaze on Mitsuba. "Do you still want to know?" she asked.

There was a long pause before Mitsuba replied, in a shaky whisper, "I . . . I do."

"No matter what the details are?"

Mitsuba swallowed hard, then nodded. "No matter what the details are!"

"Hmm. All right," Chie said. She took out the note paper she'd had Mitsuba write her family's names down on a week before and showed it to her. "Your mother is Kazene Mitsuba, and your sister is Kiyone Mitsuba, correct?" Mitsuba nodded yes. "On the day of the Idol Fest, there was an incident in an 8th Ward hospital where a terminally ill patient named Yujiro Utsumi was stabbed by his housekeeper. Afterward, the housekeeper tried to kill herself."

The day she'd first brought Mitsuba to this condo, Chie had inadvertently come across the incident while browsing news stories online. It had recently come to light that the perpetrator behind a string of incidents involving missing high school girls had been a Ghoul: Yujiro Utsumi's adopted daughter, Koharu Utsumi. These incidents apparently went back as far as eighteen years ago, with high school girls being abducted mainly from the 8th Ward and the wards neighboring it—including the 23rd, where Mitsuba had said she used to live.

"The housekeeper who stabbed Yujiro Utsumi was apparently named 'Otokaze.' " Mitsuba's mother's name was Kazene. If you switched the kanji around and changed their readings, you got "Otokaze."

"Thanks to the detective who rushed to the scene, Yujiro Utsumi survived the attack and is still alive, at least for the time being. The same detective was apparently quick enough to deal with Otokaze after she tried to kill herself; he wound up saving her life. Probably lucky that this all happened in a hospital. Anyhow, I had Ikuma get in touch with this detective for me. They discussed things behind the scenes, and he managed to get this photo of Otokaze." Chie slid the

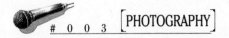

photo she'd gotten from Ikuma over to Mitsuba.

Mitsuba cried out at the sight of the emaciated woman sleeping in the bed. "Mother!" She looked nothing like the woman in the happy family photo Chie had seen before, but Mitsuba's voice confirmed it. Her mother. Tears began to stream down the girl's face.

"So this is just supposition on my part, but I think what happened is that, while your mother was looking for your sister, she ran across this Utsumi family, and she may have become their housekeeper as part of her search."

Mitsuba grabbed on to Chie's shirt and leaned in close. "Miss Hori, is there some way I can see my mother? Please, I . . . I want to see her!" While the reality of the situation was grave, it didn't change the fact that her mother was still alive. She clung to Chie, sobbing as she begged over and over again.

Seeing this, Ikuma spoke up. "The detective on this case really opened up to me after I told him about you, Mitsuba. He knew he wasn't supposed to, but he let me have this picture, and he also promised me he'd make a special exception in allowing a meeting."

"Meaning . . ."

Ikuma flashed Chie a look, and Chie smile brightly. "Meaning yes, you can see her," she replied. "Do you think now would be all right, Ikuma?"

"Hmm. Maybe? I mean the detective did say he wanted to see Mitsuba ASAP, so it's probably all right?" Ikuma got out his cell phone and started typing away to check on that.

With Ikuma focusing on that, Chie moved on to the next

matter at hand. "Mitsuba, we should use this opportunity to bail on this place and get ready to move someplace else."

Mitsuba wiped her tears away. "Yeah," she said with a nod before standing up.

Chie checked her computer one last time, but she didn't have any new emails. "I hope this won't take much longer," she said, sighing as she slipped the laptop into her backpack and hefted it up.

Ikuma made an "OK" sign with his hand. "You're good to go, Chie!"

"Mitsuba, your mother's hospital is in the 8th Ward."

"From here it's maybe thirty or forty minutes by taxi," Ikuma said.

"All right. Thank you so much!" Mitsuba said, bowing to both Chie and Ikuma.

Ikuma turned to Chie and nodded. "Ready to get going?"

When they turned toward the door, however, it was already open, and a man was standing there. "Going on a little picnic, are we? I'd be delighted if I could join you."

"Ah, geez," Chie muttered.

Ikuma's face fell. "Oh, you gotta be kidding me . . ."

Over by the back window, Mitsuba gasped, only just now noticing the intruder, doubtless recognizing him from the picture Chie had shown her previously.

The picture of Shu Tsukiyama feeding on someone.

"So you were right under my nose this whole time. To think you'd be sneaking about in my own townhouse, Hori!" Tsukiyama stepped

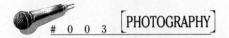

inside without bothering to
slip off his shoes, the door
behind him locking with a
sharp click as he reached
back for it. "But you've made
a clear mistake in choosing
the 23rd Ward, under heavy
guard."

Tsukiyama made gran-
diose, operatic gestures as
he spoke. "You see, knowing
you, Hori, I realized you'd
probably hide someplace I'd
have a hard time getting to.
And what place fits the bill
better than the 23rd Ward?
After that, it was a simple
matter of having my atten-
dants do some searching."

"Took you long enough,
all things considered."

"My master has been
busy searching for Kamishi-
ro, and I've been aiding him
in that. But I finally found the
time to swing by," Tsukiyama

said as he hungrily eyed Mitsuba like his prey. "Heh heh . . . Oh, I've longed to meet you, my sad little songstress! Have you been crying? I can see those charming eyes of yours wavering with tears." He slowly crept closer and closer to Mitsuba.

"Ikuma, can you take Tsukiyama in a fight?" Chie asked.

"Nuh-uh, no way! Can an amateur boxer take on the heavyweight champ? Because that's basically what you're asking here!"

Someone had to do something, though, or the girl was as good as dead.

"I'll replace your pearls of tears with rich rubies of blood . . . Oh, the very thought of it is just *thrilling*!" Tsukiyama shouted, his eyes now a flush crimson. He radiated an air of menace that made it hard to even breathe. Mitsuba slumped back onto the floor.

"I should thank you, Hori. This little ordeal you've made me go through has ratcheted my appetite up a tiny notch!" Tsukiyama's Kagune coiled around his right arm like a slithering snake, soon taking on a knifelike shape, which he brandished at Mitsuba. "This is going to be the most fun I've had with a meal in a long time!"

No ordinary person—no ordinary Ghoul, even—would be able to bring themselves to take action in the face of such a threat.

Chie turned to Ikuma and snapped, "Ikuma, jump!"

"Oh, goddammit!" Spurred into action, Ikuma's own eyes went red. Hefting Chie up over one shoulder, he then dove in next to Mitsuba. He yanked her in close with his free hand and, clutching her tight, leapt away from Tsukiyama—and right toward the window as he cried out, "This is why I hate my own peeeeeopplleeee!"

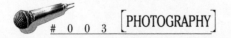

0 0 3 [PHOTOGRAPHY]

There was the piercing sound of shattering glass as he jumped right through the window, and the three of them began to plummet as gravity took over.

"Eeeeeeeek!"

"Whoa, this is aaaawesome!" Chie's playful shout intermingled with Mitsuba's terrified shriek.

Ikuma held the other two tightly and shouted, "Hold on tight!" His Kagune erupted through his skin around his shoulder blades and wrapped around his body in a spiral, reaching all the way down to his feet, where it took on a shape like a spring.

He grunted as his Kagune softened the impact of landing. It still hurt, but considering they'd just leapt from the top floor of an apartment building, it wasn't too bad at all.

"Wow, you're really good at carrying stuff!" Chie said.

"That's why I work part time for a shipping company! But hey, this isn't the time to joke around like that!"

Mitsuba seemed to have finally realized what Ikuma was. "I-Ikuma, are . . . are you a . . . ?"

"Sorry for not saying anything! I wasn't trying to deceive you. For now, let's just hope we can get away!" Ikuma quashed his Kagune and began running through the nighttime city streets. It was doubtful that Tsukiyama was just going to stand by and let them run off.

"You're not getting away that easily!" he cried as he leapt gracefully from the window.

"Ikuma," Chie asked, "how long can you hold out for us?"

"Well, I'm carrying two people, *and* I've got Tsukiyama of all people after me! I think if he wanted to, he could end this in the blink of an eye, but he's probably having more fun toying with us right now."

Clinging to Ikuma's shoulder, Chie looked back to see Tsukiyama following them some distance behind. He'd stopped using his Kagune, but his eyes still smoldered a fierce red. What Chie felt on seeing that, however, wasn't fear. "Wow, looking good, there, Tsukiyama!" A Ghoul running full-out with his eyes blazing amidst the darkness of night. Chie took up her camera and began to fire off shots as if she were smitten.

"Hey, look, check it out!" she said. "Tsukiyama makes for a good picture when he's not talking!"

"Chie, I'd *really* appreciate if you could focus on the more immediate situation!" Ikuma protested. "I mean Tsukiyama might not kill you because he likes you and all, but Mitsuba and I are kinda marked for death here!" He kicked up into the air and leapt over a fence, weaving up and down and side to side for dear life.

"Huh? Hey, I'm pretty sure he'd kill me too, when it came down to it! Like I'm pretty sure he wouldn't pass me up if he needed to eat, and he's definitely not so fond of me that he wouldn't sell me out to get something he wanted."

"Oh, that is *not* want I wanted to hear! I mean if that's the case for you, what's that say for the rest of us?" There probably wasn't much they could say or do in the face of such a fearsome foe. But that's why the weak used weapons.

Weapons only they could wield.

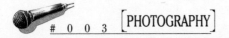 # 0 0 3 [PHOTOGRAPHY]

Chie took out her smartphone and checked her email. "Ah!" There was one new message. She tried to hold the phone steady enough to read as she bumped and jostled about. "Yes! There it is!" she cried out, unable to resist doing a quick fist pump. "Ikuma, let's get out of the 23rd Ward for now! If Ghoul investigators find us, someone like you is as good as dead!"

"Aha-hah. That'd be really sad if it weren't also so true! Okay, which way?"

"Same as the original plan: to the 8th Ward hospital!"

"Got it!" Ikuma said, picking up speed.

As if sensing that something about their situation had changed, the look on Tsukiyama's face shifted as well. "Oh, he looks so cool right now," Chie muttered. "I wish I had a better angle!" She lined Tsukiyama up in her viewfinder and clicked the shutter.

———————

Ikuma was looking understandably tired. They'd chosen a more secluded area, leapt up onto the rooftops, and kept running. Caught up in her emailing back and forth, Chie snapped back to attention as Ikuma uttered a panicked, "Uh-oh!"

Tsukiyama had closed a good chunk of the distance in one go. "Looks like it's just about checkmate!" He'd once again manifested his Kagune, his sights set directly on them.

"Sorry about this!" Ikuma said as he hurled Chie and Mitsuba into a shrub with slender, leafy branches. He crossed his now-free arms and attempted to form a shield from his kagune, but he couldn't keep up with Tsukiyama's movements.

"You weakling!"

"Agh!" Ikuma was knocked back by Tsukiyama's Kagune and slammed hard into a tree. Leaves scattered about, and a group of birds that had been resting in the branches fluttered off en masse.

"Now, then..." Tsukiyama fixed his red eyes on Mitsuba.

Ikuma managed to get back to his feet and tried to shield her, but Chie said, "It's all right, Ikuma," as she tugged her snagged clothing free of some branches and stood up.

She then faced Tsukiyama, set on trying to deal with him one final time. "Tsukiyama, I already told you, there are pictures I want to get of Mitsuba."

Tsukiyama set a hand against his chest. "Ah, Hori, my friend. We've known each other only a short time, but your feelings reach me so well it almost pains me! I would love to be able to grant your wish," he declared. "But I've been soft enough on you already!" His eyes showed not even a shadow of hesitation.

Mitsuba was visibly flustered, and Ikuma's cheeks were drawn back, but Chie couldn't really disagree with Tsukiyama's assertion, and the look on her face showed it.

"My desires need to come first. My gourmet palate needs to come first! So you'll just have to deal with that and let me fill my empty stomach. It's my God-given right!" Tsukiyama stuck a hand out to brush Chie aside. Compared to Ghouls, humans really were quite powerless. "I'll treat you to cheesecake sometime, my little mouse."

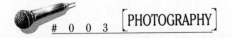

But Chie still had her secret weapon. "I'm not interested in cake right now!" She took the smartphone she'd been fiddling with earlier and held it up for him to look at it. "I know you too well, Tsukiyama."

Tsukiyama went stock-still, the text on the phone screen reflected in his eyes—a word that held a very special meaning for him.

"Kaneki"

Chie opened the email she'd gotten from him.

"Found it."

There was a sudden whoosh through the air. Tsukiyama leapt quickly back as a new presence cast its shadow where he'd stood a moment before.

His white hair fluttered, the mask on his face leaving one strangely colored eye visible. Tsukiyama looked at him, flabbergasted.

"K-Kaneki?!"

It was none other than Ken Kaneki, whom Tsukiyama had set his sights on for so long.

Ikuma, a fellow resident of the 20th Ward, was clearly puzzled. "Huh? Kaneki?" he said. "What are you doing here?"

"Chie got in contact with me. She said she had some photos I was looking for, in exchange for my doing her a favor."

"You want . . . pictures?"

"Yes. Ones necessary for my development, and which will demonstrate the atrocity of Ghouls even if I wind up getting killed," Kaneki said. Tsukiyama eyed him keenly.

"And in my quest to get interesting photos, I've got a lot of pictures of Ghouls!" Chie said. She had sold several such photos of

Ghouls to Kaneki before.

"Recently, I was able to have a little 'chat' with one of these individuals and got some very helpful information, so I thought it only fair to come and hear out Chie's request," Kaneki said, glancing down at Chie with a warm smile. "Whatever you need, just ask."

The others turned their attention to Chie, clearly wondering what she possibly wanted to ask for. She allowed herself a smile. "From now on, if you'd like to use me for something, please get in touch with me through Tsukiyama!"

That didn't seem to strike anyone as a suggestion that would resolve this situation, and the others' eyes all went wide. "You want me to get in touch with you through Tsukiyama?" Kaneki asked.

"Sure, if you think I'd be of any use to you."

"Of course. I'd certainly appreciate your assistance, but... why?"

In the back of her mind, Chie was sure that Kaneki was wondering why they'd need Tsukiyama as an intermediary when they were already in direct contact with each other. She folded her arms and said, "Because I'll be able to get much better pictures that way."

Kaneki tilted his head at first, but the smile soon returned to his face. "Very well," he said with a nod, appearing satisfied that the agreement was to Chie's benefit. "Tsukiyama," he added as he turned away from Chie and the others. "I don't know the details, but I believe Chie is on her way to take some pictures. I'd like you to see her and her friends there, *safely*." And with that, Kaneki vanished into the night.

"What is the meaning of this, Hori?" Tsukiyama asked once Kaneki was out of sight, his eyebrows raised.

"I need your help to do what's asked of me, Tsukiyama. Which means you're that much more valuable now, right? I mean it's not like I've asked for anything that'll inconvenience you."

Chie had gotten in touch with Kaneki first thing in the interest of helping Mitsuba escape. She'd figured that if she could curry favor with Kaneki by being useful, she could get Tsukiyama to give up his claim on Mistuba. And now, Tsukiyama could use Chie as a means of getting closer to Kaneki.

Tsukiyama, clever was he was, had probably weighed his options on the spot and realized which choice benefited him more. "Heh heh heh... Aha ha ha hah! Oh, you're as clever as ever, you sneaky little rodent!" After he stopped laughing, his eyes narrowed to crescent slits. "Not bad."

The issue had been resolved. "Man, I'm exhausted!" Chie said as she stretched her arms out. She then pointed her camera in the direction Kaneki had vanished and peered through the finder, muttering, "I totally get how you got so obsessed, Tsukiyama."

"As my master has directed, I'll see you there safely," Tsukiyama said.

"The safest way would be if you weren't with us," Chie said in defiance of propriety.

"Ha ha ha. You really are a unique one," Tsukiyama chuckled. "Then I shall go and ask Kaneki more details about what he'd like you to look into for him." And with that, he departed, leaving the

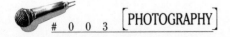

0 0 3 [PHOTOGRAPHY]

others with a sense of relief at long last.

When Chie, Ikuma, and Mitsuba finally arrived at the hospital, the detective was there, wreathed in the scent of cigarette smoke. When he spotted Mitsuba, he approached her and asked, "Are you Kotone Mitsuba, miss?"

"Yes."

"And is it correct that your older sister, Kiyone Mitsuba, went missing nine years ago, and that your mother is Kazene Mitsuba?"

"Yes, that's . . . that's right."

Hearing that, the detective took something out of his coat pocket and showed it to Mitsuba. "This was among your mother's belongings. Do you have any idea why that might be?"

In the detective's hand was a toy microphone. Mitsuba's lips trembled. "My . . . my sister loved that thing since she was little. She always carried it around with her as a sort of good-luck charm."

A sorrowful look crossed the detective's face. "I see . . ." he murmured. He then spoke briefly with some of the hospital staff before heading toward the patient rooms. "This way."

He led them to a private room deeper within the hospital. The curtains were drawn, and it was dark, but the detective switched on the light near the pillow.

"Mother!" Mitsuba gasped as the light shone on the woman's face. The girl drew herself in close, but whether because her mother's condition was too poor or because she was simply sleeping, she gave no response.

The detective launched into an explanation. "A Ghoul named

Koharu Utsumi, who'd kidnapped high school girls on the orders of Yujiro Utsumi, left behind the belongings of her victims. And not just those belonging to your sister, Kiyone Mitsuba."

Mitsuba was sobbing so heavily that she may not even have heard him. Nevertheless, he continued. "But thanks to you, we now know your mother had one of your late sister's belongings in her possession. Apparently, your mother acted as Koharu Utsumi's caretaker and was quite fond of her. Perhaps she developed some affection for her while working for the Utsumi household."

The sound of Mitsuba crying filled the small room as the detective spoke. "Perhaps Koharu realized that one of the high school girls she'd abducted had been her caretaker's daughter, and had confessed by giving back one of her belongings. Your mother had a large sum of money set aside in order to make a getaway. Maybe Koharu gave her the microphone and told her to run, but your mother..." The detective stopped short, and then bowed his head deeply toward Mitsuba. "I'm sorry I wasn't able to stop your mother."

Mitsuba, still clinging to her mother, slowly looked back up and then shook her head slightly. "Detective, you saved my mother after she tried to kill herself. I'd never have been able to see her again if not for that... I'm so happy to have even this."

Mitsuba took her mother's hand and pressed it against her cheek. Tears ran down her mother's fingers, and Mitsuba's breath washed over her skin.

"... right?" The voice was so quiet that it almost escaped notice. Surprised, everyone in the room looked around to see who had

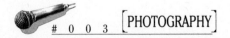
0 0 3 [PHOTOGRAPHY]

spoken, only to find that Mitsuba's mother, who'd seemingly been asleep, had opened her eyes ever so slightly.

"Mother!"

"What are... you doing here?" It was now clearly her mother who spoke. Tears were welling up in her eyes.

"Mom? Do you... Do you know who I am?" Mitsuba asked, clutching her mother's hand in hers.

"Of course I do," her mother replied, nodding several times before saying, "You're Kiyone..."

The detective started to correct her. "No, that's—"

Mitsuba waved a hand to cut him off. "Yes, that's right," she told her mother with a smile. "I'm sorry for worrying you, mom. But I became an idol singer. I'm not famous or anything yet, but I made my dream come true! That's why I came to see you, mom!" She clutched the toy microphone in her hand, a determined gleam set in her eyes. "Will you be one of my fans?"

Tears were streaming from her mother's eyes. "Of course I will," she replied.

Mitsuba embraced her mother tightly. "Thank you, mom," she said.

Her mother showed a smile of utter relief at those words, and then slipped back into sleep. As she breathed gently, Mitsuba watched her with unwavering determination in her eyes.

She had clearly made some sort of decision.

Chie felt goosebumps all over her body. This was that sensation, that moment she'd been waiting for. Quietly, she readied her camera.

"From today onward," Mitsuba said, "I will be 'Kiyone.'"

Tears fell from her eyes as she spoke, and Chie clicked the shutter in order to capture that perfect moment.

V

"Whew! Well, that sure was quite the ordeal," Chie said, back at the condo, thinking back on things as she stared at one of her photos on her computer—the photo of Mitsuba's teary-eyed face. She'd gone through quite a bit to get that picture.

Apparently, Mitsuba's mother's memories were muddled. In addition to thinking that Mitsuba was her deceased older sister, she'd apparently forgotten about Mitsuba herself. Perhaps the hardships she'd been through had altered her recollections.

As Chie puttered about on her computer, an exasperated sigh broke the silence of the room. She turned to see Tsukiyama standing there. This *was* his condo, after all. He stepped inside without bothering to ask permission.

"Don't worry. I'll leave as soon as my phone's finished charging," Chie said as she chewed on some candy she'd gotten from Ikuma.

"No can do, I'm afraid," Tsukiyama said. "Kaneki has a request for you, Hori."

Kaneki, a man so exquisitely unbalanced that people couldn't help but be drawn to him. Chie got to her feet. "Is that so?" she muttered. "Well, guess I'd better get to it!"

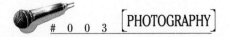

0 0 3 [PHOTOGRAPHY]

Chie called up the mental image of Kaneki in her mind.

She was certain that, someday, she'd be able to take a great picture of him.

TOKYO

東 京 ———

[VOID]

—— 喰 種 ——

GHOUL

[THE TIES THAT WOUND]

*T**his is something I can do for both of them.*

Hinami heard the door open and shut with a clunk. She jumped to her feet from the sofa, where she had been lying down. While she'd been waiting, she'd been thinking about a lot of things. *She must be lonely and sad too. Just like me.* Hinami was at a loss as to how to fill this hole. *But when we're together she seems a little distracted.*

"Touka!" Hinami exclaimed, clinging to Touka, who had just come out of her room. She buried her head in her chest. Touka gave her hair a stroke. Hinami looked up and saw that Touka was quietly smiling.

"What's up with you, Hinami?" Touka said, and gave her a worried look. Concealing her own emotions, her face was one of pure concern for Hinami. "Wanna play a game?" she said, and went into the living room.

Hinami watched her walk off and started twisting her own shirt in her hands.

II

After the Aogiri battle, there had been an oppressive air hanging over Anteiku, although everyone had made it through safely. Perhaps the missing "piece" was much larger than themselves.

"Irimi, is Mr. Yoshimura all right?" Hinami asked, seeing Irimi coming out of the room where Yoshimura, the manager of Anteiku, was recuperating. Yoshimura had singlehandedly fought the CCG elites in order to buy time while they were rescuing Kaneki. He was heavily wounded.

Irimi gave her a gentle smile. "He's just resting up so he can get better, so don't worry," she said.

"Oh. Will he get better soon?"

"Definitely. He'll have the café up and going again in no time."

Anteiku was temporarily closed at the moment. The door was shut, and the café, which was usually filled with a gentle buzz, was deserted.

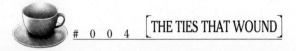 # 0 0 4 [THE TIES THAT WOUND]

But Koma, the big-nosed waiter who had been left in charge of the store while it was closed, was keeping things in good order so that the café could be reopened at any time. And the rooms that had been destroyed in the Aogiri attack were still being repaired and would soon be restored to their former state.

"I guess you and Touka are gonna be really busy," Hinami said casually. A faint shadow passed over Irimi's face.

"Hinami, how's Touka doing?"

"Um, well . . . same as always," she answered.

Touka had gone into battle against the Aogiri Tree, fully prepared to die in order to save Kaneki, who had been kidnapped and imprisoned by them. Hinami thought that nobody had wanted to rescue Kaneki more than Touka, the young woman who let Hinami call her "big sister."

She was often rather cold when it came to Kaneki, but she worried about him more than anyone else.

Hinami remembered seeing Touka immediately after Kaneki was kidnapped by Aogiri, pale-faced and shaking a little as Yoshimura told her that she should consider the fact that she may never see Kaneki again.

Bring Kaneki back and get back to normal. That was what everyone had wanted.

Hinami couldn't fight like Touka could, but she'd learned from Irimi how to use her senses and had joined the fight by supporting everyone else. And then finally they'd succeeded in finding Kaneki, but—

It was like a novel by Sen Takatsuki, Hinami's favorite author. There had been a conflict over something—conflicted emotions, misunderstood feelings, and a longed-for conclusion that never came to pass.

"Now things can go back to normal," Touka had said, but Kaneki rejected that notion.

"I'm not going back to Anteiku."

That was not all. Touka wanted to follow Kaneki if he was going to go his own way and do what he wanted to do, but he had rejected those feelings as well.

And then he'd taken off and left her there.

It must have been quite a shock for her, Hinami thought. *And I'm sure it still hurts.* But it wasn't something she ever talked about in front of Hinami. And that made Hinami desperately sad.

What can I do to cheer her up?

Everyone was gathered in the entrance room, as if something was happening. When Hinami walked in, their pet cockatiel Hetare sang, "Hetare, hetare!" Hinami realized that this was the day of the week when Kaneki would usually give Hetare food, so she got the food out and changed his water. Hetare—whose name meant "loser"—buried his head in his food tray, pecking at his food like it might disappear soon.

She pulled a chair over by Hetare's cage and watched him. Hetare started hopping around on his perch. *Maybe he's anxious because I'm here.*

"I wonder how Kaneki's doing . . ."

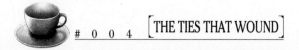 # 0 0 4 [THE TIES THAT WOUND]

Touka wasn't the only one she was worried about. She was also concerned about Kaneki, who had gone and left them.

Hinami hadn't gotten to speak to him before he left that day, but watching from a distance she thought he looked lonely as he walked away, and that thought had stayed with her.

None of that changes the fact that they care about each other. So why do they both have to be so sad?

Hinami stood up, then put her finger through a gap in the bird's cage. Hetare took note immediately and pressed his red cheek to her finger, playfully pretending to scratch his head against her. When she started to gently scratch his head with her fingernail, the overexcited bird looked at her happily. *That's probably enough,* Hinami thought. She pulled her hand away and had started to walk out of the room when Hetare squealed, "Hetare, hetare!"

"I'll come back later," Hinami said, and shut the door. Hetare was still squawking.

She slipped secretly into the café. Even though it was temporarily closed, the store still smelled like fragrant coffee. Every time she took a breath the taste of coffee in the air made her tongue dance.

"Oh, we've got a customer. A cute one, too."

A jolt of surprise went through Hinami. She had thought she was alone, but Koma was standing behind the counter. She thought he would be mad at her for coming in without permission, but Koma went back to work without telling her off.

"Mr. Koma, what are you doing?"

"Checking the coffee machine. Has to be done at a time

like this."

With practiced movements, Koma busily dismantled the device and wiped down its interior workings, replacing parts as needed. Hinami sat down at the counter and watched. Then, as if something had just occurred to him, he started brewing coffee with the machine he'd just checked.

Compared to the scent of coffee that lingered in the store, it smelled so rich that it tickled Hinami's nose.

"Here you go," Koma said, pouring the coffee into a cup and handing it over the counter to Hinami.

"Oh, are you sure?"

"I think the café feels lonely too, without any customers here."

Hinami looked around her.

"Can a café be lonely?"

"It sure can. A café is like the cup, and customers are the coffee. One is not complete without the other. So I'm sure the café misses having people in it. Well, drink up, before it goes cold," Koma said.

Hinami brought the coffee up to her mouth.

Coffee was the only thing she could have without feeling a sense of guilt, and it was also one of the very few things that Ghouls could share with humans. The coffee that Koma had made smelled somehow friendly. With each sip she remembered when the café was crowded. Hinami turned to look around again.

"You know, Kaneki used to come here a lot before he started working here."

"Really?!"

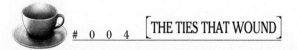

0 0 4 [THE TIES THAT WOUND]

"Yeah. I think he really liked the coffee I make."

"Oh... Maybe he still misses your coffee..." she murmured, and Koma smiled.

"You're worried about him, aren't you?"

"Yeah."

"I'm worried about him too. I wonder if the people in his group feel they can't stop him even if he's being reckless... But then, I don't know if it'd be any different if I were there."

"What do you mean, can't stop him?" She tilted her head, unable to understand what he meant. Koma gave her a know-it-all look.

"The people who are following Kaneki see him as a 'leader.' His word is law, and they'd risk their lives for him. But they can't tell him when he's doing something wrong, or get angry with him, without consequences."

"Why? Don't they all like Kaneki?"

"That's what happens when you're a leader. It's always lonely at the top, no matter how many friends you have."

Hinami tilted her head to one side again, so Koma spoke in more detail.

"When there's a power imbalance, it's impossible to stand on an equal footing. Those who are higher up don't want to make everyone anxious, so they have no choice but to take a strong stance on everything, and those who are lower down have to be strong and accept everything the leader says."

"Is that... what it's like?"

"Yeah. Touka could sometimes stop him from lashing out, but

the people around him now can't do anything but look on, I imagine."

As she listened, Hinami became increasingly anxious.

"I wonder if he's all right. . ."

"Oh, but the thing is, a strong bond develops between people who fight together. I don't think you need to worry about him, Hinami," Koma rushed to add.

Just then the front door swung open, even though the café was temporarily closed.

"Sorry, we're closed tod—"

But Koma stopped in the middle of his sentence.

"Nishiki? Shouldn't you be in class?"

Standing at the door was Nishio Nishiki, a member of staff at the Anteiku and a student at the same college as Kaneki.

"No afternoon classes today. Any word on me getting some shifts soon?" he said, walking up to the seats at the counter.

"I think we should reopen soon. Yoshimura is still taking it easy, so I can't say anything for certain."

"Really. . ." Nishiki said, hesitantly. There was nothing for him to do there, but he didn't seem to want to leave. He started muttering, "Hmm. . . . Well, what can you do, huh?" under his breath. Suddenly Hinami realized something.

"You're worried about Kaneki too, aren't you?"

Frowning, he stuttered, "W-what? No, no way." Koma grinned and rubbed his chin.

"Why are you grinning, Koma?"

"Well, well, Nishiki. Let me get you some coffee. I'll make

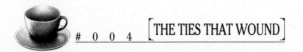

0 0 4 [THE TIES THAT WOUND]

it slowly."

"I don't really want one . . ."

"No, let me," Koma said and started making him a cup. Nishiki sat down next to Hinami at the counter, looking disappointed.

"Here you go."

Nishiki took a gulp of steaming hot coffee and looked around the café like he was searching for an escape route. Koma looked more and more amused. The atmosphere in the café felt a little better now. But then Irimi appeared.

"May I see you for a minute?"

Apparently she had a task for Koma.

"Too bad," teased Koma. "I was just about to commiserate with Nishio here about our worries over Kaneki's whereabouts."

"I told you, I'm not worried!"

Nishiki slammed his hand down on the counter, and Koma disappeared into the back of the café, grinning. Nishiki put his head on his hands sulkily and drank

his coffee. It was just Hinami and Nishiki now. They sat there in the strangely quiet café.

"Hey, brat," Nishiki muttered, breaking the silence. His head was still turned away from her as he spoke. "How's that ugly girl you live with?"

"Ugly girl?"

"Touka, I'm talking about Touka."

Hinami stared up at him, blinking her big eyes. Stung by her gaze, Nishiki jumped slightly and stammered, "W-what?"

"So you're worried about Touka, too."

"Huh?! Where'd you get that?"

"But . . ."

"I'm not!" he yelled, desperately denying it. But little Hinami made Nishiki feel truly pathetic for making excuses. He sighed deeply and stopped shouting.

Then he started spilling out words.

"Kaneki hasn't gone to any of his classes."

"He's not going to school?"

"It's like he's just dropped out of human society."

Nishiki put his cup down on the saucer, then threw his head back and looked up at the ceiling.

"I knew that bastard was trying to find 'the right distance away from people,' but once he saw those dangerous Ghouls his goal totally changed. His cherished idea of finding the right distance away from people just went straight out the window."

Hinami wondered if he was actually talking to her, or if he was

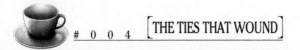

0 0 4 [THE TIES THAT WOUND]

just saying it to confirm it for himself.

He lowered his eyes to his coffee and brought it up to his lips.

"He still doesn't fully get how hard it is for Ghouls like us to get into human society. It's like dominoes: if one goes down, they all go. And once you lose it, it doesn't come back that easily," he said. "God, what a stupid bastard."

Nishiki finished his coffee and stood up.

"Look, brat, finish your coffee and get out of here."

"Oh, um . . ."

Hinami drained the little bit of coffee left in the bottom of her cup and passed it to Nishiki. He rolled up his sleeves and started to wash the cups with familiar motions.

"Things seem all right here . . ."

Nishiki wiped the cups dry and put them back on the shelf. "Bye," he said and left the café.

It was difficult for Hinami to understand all of what Nishiki had said. But one thing she did understand was that he was jealously guarding the place where he felt he belonged.

And Kaneki's the one who gave him that opportunity.

———————

That evening, when Touka was finished at school, she came back to Anteiku.

"Hina, I'm back."

She was covered in scratches and still not back to her normal strength, but she didn't seem to have any problem going to school.

"Mr. Koma made me some coffee today."

"That's nice. He makes great coffee, doesn't he?"

Hinami sat beside Touka, going over the day's events. Touka listened, chipping in occasionally.

"I think Nishiki's worried about big brother too."

"I didn't think he was that kind of guy."

"No, but he is. He knows a lot about big brother. He said he's still not going to his classes."

Touka said nothing.

"I wonder where he is right now . . . I wish he'd come visit." She looked up at Touka, who was staring into the distance as if she were grappling with something.

Big sister . . .

Did I make her sadder by talking about Kaneki?

"Big sister, hold my hand," she said cheerfully to change the subject.

"Oh, right," Touka said, and held out her hand. Hinami put her hand in Touka's, and like always, Touka squeezed her hand. *It makes me happy, so why am I so sad?*

When I'm upset, Touka is always there for me and cares for me

0 0 4 [THE TIES THAT WOUND]

more than anyone else. But now, when she's overwhelmed and her
heart and body are wounded, there's nothing I can do for her.

I love Touka and Kaneki. If I could make a wish, I'd ask for the
strength of two people so I could help. But to them I'm just a kid, not
somebody they can rely on.

That's why, like Koma said, we're not "equal."

III

It had been over two months since Kaneki had disappeared.
Anteiku reopened, and at first glance everyone seemed to have gotten back to their usual routines. Little by little, they stopped talking
about Kaneki. That made Hinami a little scared.

Touka had recently been doing things like buying reference
books or going to the library to study with her friend Yoriko. She had
started preparing in earnest for her college entrance exams.

Hinami liked reading the books Touka bought to learn words
and kanji she didn't know. *The more I learn, the more I want to learn.*

Hinami didn't know how awful exams could be because she
didn't go to school, but she thought it was great that Touka was trying to gain more knowledge.

But Touka didn't throw herself into studying when she was
around Hinami. She made sure not to stay too late studying at the
library, and always got home to see Hinami.

Devoting herself to studying had given her back a little of her old energy. Having a goal seemed to be good for her.

But Touka almost never spoke about Kaneki anymore. *Is she giving in to the passage of time and forgetting all about him?*

"So just wait in the back until I'm done."

"All right!"

Touka was on shift that day. Hinami, who had come to Anteiku with her, happily put some new food in Hetare's dish. It was her week to take care of Hetare, a duty that rotated among everyone, Kaneki excluded.

The rooms that had been destroyed by Aogiri had been perfectly rebuilt and looked just the same as ever.

Hinami sat down on the sofa and started reading her book, so as not to get in anyone's way.

"What's that character?"

As she read, she came across some difficult kanji, but she quickly figured out how to read them.

That says "downpour."

In her mind she heard Kaneki's kindly voice, telling her what the words meant.

"Oh . . ."

At the same time, she heard the sound of footsteps. She raised her head, closed her book, and followed the noise out into the hallway.

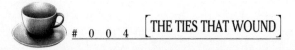 # 0 0 4 [THE TIES THAT WOUND]

Standing there was Renji Yomo, who seemed surprised to see Hinami. He looked down at her for a second, then tried to pass by.

Hinami gathered her courage. "Um, sorry," she said to stop him. Yomo paused, his back turned to her.

"Is Kaneki . . . all right, do you know?" she asked. Yomo looked back; his face was blank.

"Why are you asking me?" he said.

"I just thought, since you know about everything . . ."

"You've overestimated me," he said shortly, trying to end the conversation.

"B-but you *do* know where he is, don't you!" She kept hounding him.

"How'd you hear that?"

"Please . . . I care about him. I love Kaneki, and I only want to hear about him because I'm worried. And I think maybe if Touka heard he's doing well, it might put her mind at ease . . . ."

Yomo finally turned to look at Hinami, who was now hiding her face. But he said nothing. Perhaps he wanted to say something, but the words wouldn't come.

"I want to know when he'll achieve what he wants to. And if he'll come back here when he's done. And then maybe we can—"

—*all be together again.*

"Should I just wait here? Wait here with big sister?"

Once again Yomo said nothing. *I bet he wouldn't tell me anything*

 # 0 0 4 [THE TIES THAT WOUND]

anyway. Hinami slumped and started walking reluctantly back to the living room.

"Just wait here," Yomo muttered quietly. Hinami turned around, surprised. She didn't think he'd say anything. She waited for him to finish the sentence, but Yomo left without saying another word.

Just wait here...

Were the next words, "what else can you do?"

Even after Touka finished her shift and they walked home together, Hinami stayed lost in thought. Yomo's words just kept playing over and over in her head.

He knows how Kaneki's doing. I know he does. So since he told me "Just wait here," that must mean there's a small chance that Kaneki might come back.

"Hinami? You all right?"

She was sitting on the sofa, knees to her chest, with a hard expression on her face. Touka sat down next to her and leaned in, peeking at Hinami's face.

"It's nothing!" she said, but Touka still looked worried.

"Really?"

"Yeah, really."

It made Hinami happy and embarrassed that Touka was worried about her, and she threw her arms around Touka, who smiled wryly at this show of affection and gave her a few pats on the back. When things were good like this, Hinami's worries started to fade little by little. She started to feel more comfortable, and her eyelids fluttered heavily. Remembering the warmth of her mother, Ryoko, who had died protecting her, Hinami drifted into the land of sleep.

0 0 4 [THE TIES THAT WOUND]

I had a dream.

Big brother?

A dream where Kaneki was in a place so, so far away that I could barely make out his shape.

I yelled out, "Big brother!" But he was so far away that my voice didn't reach him. I tried to run toward him but it was like my feet were glued to the ground.

Hesitantly, I found my voice again and yelled, "Big brother!" But Kaneki was getting farther and farther away. Before long I couldn't see him anymore, and I was left behind, all alone.

Then, suddenly, Touka appeared instead.

"Big sister . . ."

Finally I could move again. "I just saw him," I said, grabbing Touka's hand, but even though she was so close she didn't react to what I said. But she was staring sadly toward where Kaneki had been. I called out again and again and pulled her hand, but she didn't look at me. She just kept looking far away.

"Mm . . ."

Hinami's eyes fluttered open and, her mind still hazy from sleep, she looked around. The light was still on, and a blanket had been draped over her.

She turned over and looked up to find Touka there. She had fallen asleep on her, using her knee as a pillow.

"Big sister?"

Touka's eyes were closed, and she was slumped back on the sofa. From her regular breathing, it was clear that she was asleep too.

When she took another look, she saw a biology textbook lying in Touka's hand. *I guess she was studying while I was asleep.*

"Mmm..." muttered Touka quietly. *I guess she's waking up because I moved.* Reflexively, Hinami pretended to still be asleep.

"Wha... Oh God, I fell asleep...."

Touka stretched a little and adjusted the blanket covering Hinami. Then she picked up her book and started flipping through it.

Hinami opened her eyes a sliver and stole a glance at Touka.

"Oh, I have so much to remember..." she murmured, sounding fed up, but she didn't put down the book. Touka squinted and furrowed her brow, trying hard to understand what she was reading. *Does she always look like this when she studies?*

It was hard for Hinami to keep pretending she was asleep because she wanted to talk to Touka. *I want to tell her about the scary dream I just had.*

But Touka kept reading until, suddenly, she looked up at the ceiling as if she'd just remembered something, and sighed.

Hinami couldn't really see her face from where she was lying. Just as she wondered what was going on, Hinami heard Touka talking to herself quietly.

"Damnit, Kaneki..."

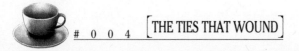 # 0 0 4 [THE TIES THAT WOUND]

Her voice was tinged with both anger and sorrow.

She muttered those words, then silently stood and picked up Hinami in her arms. Then she carried Hinami to bed, said, "Good night," and left.

Hinami lay there quietly until she was sure Touka had gone.

Then she slowly got out of bed. The door was closed. The light in the living room was off, and Touka had apparently gone back to her room.

"Touka? Big sister?" she said, so quietly it could not be heard. Hinami closed her eyes tightly, hoping to forget. But the voice was burned in her mind, and it kept coming back to her again and again.

Touka tried so hard to be cheerful in front of Hinami, but her pain still came through.

She hadn't forgotten Kaneki at all. She thought about him nearly every day, but she kept the pain to herself and never let it show on the outside. *But still, she finds things that she needs to do for herself, and it's a slow journey she's learning from.*

As she thought about Touka, Hinami realized something. Or rather, she felt an inkling about something.

"I'm getting in her way..."

Touka had never thought of Hinami as an annoyance, and Hinami had never suspected that she had. She believed in Touka. She knew that they would always be together.

But I'm tying her down.

She never neglects me to focus on her studies. And no matter how much she needs to study, no matter how busy she is with school, she always gives me precedence, sacrificing herself for me.

And it's always been like this. Once Kaneki disappeared she was consumed by such deep sadness, but still she always tucks me into bed at night.

Looking back now, Hinami remembered how Touka always worried about her whenever she remembered Kaneki and felt sad, pushing down her own sadness.

It's because she thinks I need to be protected. It makes me so happy I could cry, but it hurts with every breath because I'm crying.

Just like my mother, who protected me at the cost of her own life, Touka does all she can to support me—even pushing down her own feelings. I can't do anything for her. I'm just baggage. Hinami clenched her shirt in her fists and bit her lip.

"Big brother..."

If he'd just come back this feeling would all go away in a second. And Touka wouldn't have to call out so sadly.

But in the end, that's just waiting in vain for someone else to save me.

Hinami remembered how Kaneki had looked as he said goodbye to Touka after the battle with Aogiri. *Lonely. I wonder if he's still fighting even now. I wonder if that gentle, book-loving boy is out there shedding blood, gouging through flesh, and taking someone's life away. If he'll ever be able to find his way back home.*

And then, with nowhere to turn back to, where would he go on his own?

"No, it can't be..."

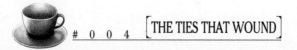 # 0 0 4 [THE TIES THAT WOUND]

She remembered the dream she'd just had, and how he hadn't heard her calling to him. How he'd disappeared into the darkness alone.

She let go of her shirt and brought her hands together so firmly that she thought her fingertips might break.

My hands are much smaller and weaker than Touka's and Kaneki's. And I know I can't do much with them. But living here, in a safe place where I'm taken care of and can have a comfortable life, my voice can't reach anyone. That's how it stands.

Hinami thought for a moment.

If someone can't hear you, you need to go closer. If your words don't reach them, you grab their hand.

And when Kaneki is alone and lost, there's something I want to tell him. That he'll always have a way home, and somewhere to return to. That I'll get lost with him, because I don't want him to be alone.

Maybe being with him would hurt me, but the pain of being protected eventually makes one spoiled and corrupted.

I want to tell Kaneki, dressed in his lonely armor, that there are people nearby who care about him. I want to tell him that Touka is waiting for him to come back.

Because I know, more than anyone else, that nobody can go through life on their own.

"I want to protect them too—big brother and big sister!"

Listen. Latch on to the sound. It takes human form in your mind and tells you where you belong.

In an abandoned building, one left vacant since going bankrupt a few years ago, Hinami's hands were on the floor of the lobby, her arms outstretched. Kaneki and Kazuichi Banjo, along with Ichimi, Jiro, and Sante—a close band of guys who wanted to put their energies to use and carry out actions with Kaneki—stood holding their breath and watching.

"Hasn't noticed us yet . . ."

"On the third floor, possibly in the little room close to the stairs . . . asleep."

Kaneki looked toward the stairs, then pointed to Ichimi and Jiro. They nodded.

Then Kaneki pointed to the floor, indicating to Banjo and Sante to stay there. Sante nodded obediently, but Banjo, who had taken a vow to shield Kaneki and had been with him all this time, looked chagrined.

Banjo was as muscular as a professional wrestler, and he appeared strong at first glance, but he could not release a Kagune. And without a Kagune it was impossible to battle other Ghouls.

So for now, he would fight against Ghouls given to him by Chie Hori, the informer with some connection to Tsukiyama.

"I think he's perfect for Kaneki to take on."

He looked at the photos she'd sent and said, "This is Noyama."

0 0 4 [THE TIES THAT WOUND]

After his parents were killed by the CCG, he palmed his beautiful younger sister off to a millionaire and turned her into a bit of a money-spinner. He told people his plan was to wait until the millionaire died, when the money would go to his sister, but his sister had recently been killed by the CCG.

Kaneki had gone one flight up the stairs. He snapped his fingers. Then he dashed off all at once.

By the count of ten there was a roar from the floor above.

"Here we go!"

Then, the sound of something hitting the wall and a vibration.

"H-Hinami, what should we do?" Banjo asked worriedly, but Hinami answered, "It's all right, that wasn't Kaneki." A rain of dust fell from the ceiling.

All this banging and thumping was hurting Hinami's ears.

"Tsukiyama wanted to be here for this too," Sante said. But today Tsukiyama was out lending support to Chie Hori because she was getting to the heart of the information gathering that Kaneki had asked her to do.

Her current goal was to find the list of fugitives from Cochlea. And the outcome of their war largely rested on whether or not she could get this information.

"Tsukiyama's dangerous. And Kaneki doesn't want to show his hand right now."

Known as "Kaneki's sword," Tsukiyama held a completely different position among Kaneki's followers than Banjo, but sometimes that "sword" took a few practice swings that may or may not have been aimed at Kaneki. Nor did Kaneki appear to completely trust Tsukiyama. But his ability could not be overstated. In fact, there were lots of things that couldn't go ahead without Tsukiyama, which drove Banjo crazy.

"Whoa."

Another roar, louder than any other roar had been. "Is it over?" Sante whispered.

But Hinami had reached a very different conclusion.

"It's coming from the stairs! They're getting away!"

The roar was the sound of a Ghoul being slammed back into the part of the stairs that connected two floors.

If Noyama had taken the blow, then he might try running away. And if that happened—

"We gotta go! He's gonna come here!"

At the same time Banjo yelled, Sante picked up Hinami and started running.

Banjo ran toward the stairs with the intention of serving as backup.

"Gzzzzzooooooooooooooooooooonnnnn!"

Noyama came flying down the stairs, as Hinami had guessed, making a strange screeching sound as he did. His Kagune was an ukaku, perfect for high-speed attacks. Banjo, who had wanted to try to buy a little time until Hinami could escape from the abandoned building, was blown back instantly, making it impossible to buy even a second of time.

"Banjo!"

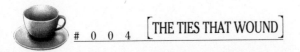 # 0 0 4 [THE TIES THAT WOUND]

"Expected nothing less from you, Banjo!"

Sante ran at full speed with Hinami in his arms, unconcerned about Banjo, perhaps because he had never counted on him at all. Recognizing Hinami and Sante as Kaneki's friends and, furthermore, seeing that they were not blessed with a lot of fighting power, Noyama vengefully reduced the distance between them in one burst. Noyama was catching up with Hinami and Sante much faster than they could make it to the door of the abandoned building.

"No!"

Noyama's Kagune was close. But Hinami heard the unmistakable buzzing sound of Rc cells being released, followed by the sound of someone falling to the floor.

"Sante, leave him to Kaneki!"

He reacted immediately to Hinami's words and kicked the ground.

Noyama's body rose up with the force of the blow, nearly hitting the ceiling, and in that second Kaneki's Kagune speared him. *If Noyama had been running in front of us, we would've been speared too.*

"Whoaaaaa, wow!" shouted Sante admiringly, rotating and landing skillfully.

Now Noyama can't run away again. Now all he can do is wait to die. But Hinami, who was back on her own two feet again, still couldn't run over to Kaneki's side.

"You did some quite heartless things, didn't you?"

Kaneki sounded cold as he spoke to Noyama, who was twitching like a bug with its wings plucked off.

"Kaneki, you got something on him?"

"Lots of photos of him dismantling girls. Where's Banjo?"

"Laid out over there. When Banjo saw the pictures he freaked out."

While Ichimi and the others talked casually, Hinami remembered the first time she had met Kaneki.

She remembered asking him whether he was a human or a Ghoul because of the mysterious smell he gave off.

And Kaneki had told her that his body was part Ghoul but his mind was human. And that if he could, he would go back to having a human body.

"Gotta separate the wheat from the chaff," Kaneki said, snapping open the mouth restraint on his mask and biting down on Noyama's ukaku.

"Aieeeeeoooooo!"

A pain like Noyama had never experienced made him jump and twitch.

Kaneki has fully crossed the line and jumped into the Ghoul world.

But now that he's decided to accept that he's a Ghoul and live as one, when will he realize?

Hinami could still smell it—the human scent that clung to his body. *It'll always be with him.*

Now that he's turned his sights away from being a human, he must be scared that a day will come when he'll be punished as a human.

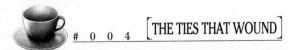 # 0 0 4 [THE TIES THAT WOUND]

Hinami remembered something else—the day that Kaneki had told Touka that he wanted to go back to how he was.

———————

I thought, if he's dangerous, then maybe he should be stopped. I thought someone should warn him about what would happen if he carried on. And even if she gets angry at me and tells me not to be so stupid, that's fine.

But instead, silence. Touka just sat there looking at Hinami. Hinami stared straight back at her.

"I see."

At last, Touka smiled wryly.

"When you look at me like that, what can I even say?"

She turned away from Hinami's gaze and was silent for a while, but eventually she looked straight back at Hinami.

"You can always come back."

She didn't say anything else. Touka reached out and hugged Hinami tightly, as if she was trying not to lose her, and Hinami hugged her back with all of her strength.

I really want to be here with Touka. I don't want to leave. But right now I'm just weighing her down.

———————

"You done?" Ichimi muttered, looking at Kaneki, who had

stepped away from Noyama's body.

There was something about Kaneki, who was now done fighting, that kept anyone from approaching him. *I don't know whether that's his intention or just a figment of our imagination.*

But Hinami rushed over to Kaneki anyway, calling for him.

"Big brother!"

His hair had turned white, his nails had turned dark red, and his heart was grief-stricken—everyone agreed he had changed.

But he was always kind to Hinami. He was one of the most important people to her because he had saved her, and that would never change.

Kaneki turned to look. He was bathed in someone else's blood, but he smiled gently and said, "You didn't get hurt, did you, Hinami?"

We are with you, Hinami whispered to him in her mind. *Me, and Touka too. Even if I can't get it across to you now, I want to prove to you that we're with you.*

"Yeah, I'm fine! Let's go home, big brother."

Kaneki smiled. "Yep, let's go," he said and started walking.

"We have to move to another Ward now."

Tomorrow is another day on this rocky path we walk, never knowing stability. But I believe.

I believe that the sun shines after a downpour.

 # 0 0 4 $\left[\text{THE TIES THAT WOUND}\right]$

[MISATO]

Even investigators fall in love.

In the 13th Ward, under the command of Special Class Investigator Iwao Kuroiwa, a meeting had just adjourned, the assembled Ghoul investigators looked on in astonishment at what they'd been presented with.

In the center was the 13rd Ward's sole female Ghoul investigator, Misato Gori, with her slender frame and mole set between her eyebrows. She had a slightly disagreeable look in her eyes, but that was par for the course with her. She was currently a rank 2 investigator, and had just recently taken part in the Aogiri conflict, providing successful long-range fire support with her ukaku Quinque, Emelio.

"I brought you all a little something," Misato said, somehow bashful, as she reached into her bag and set the plate of black, lumpy, burnt-smelling *somethings* on the table. The others were unable to take their eyes off them.

"Misato, what are these?"

"They're doughnuts!"

Right. Sure they were.

With the exception of Kuroiwa, the investigators screamed internally. Try though they might, it was hard to see the offerings as anything more burnt lumps of dough that had been reduced nearly to cinders.

Kuroiwa, however, reached out, took one in hand, and tossed it into his mouth.

"S-sir?!"

"Mr. Kuroiwa!"

Despite the panicked shouts of the onlooking investigators fill-

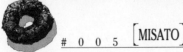

0 0 5 [MISATO]

ing the room, the crunching, crumbling sounds coming from within Kuroiwa's mouth were still clearly audible, suggesting something that, to say nothing of qualifying as a doughnut, didn't even qualify as food.

But Kuroiwa chewed thoroughly, swallowed it down, and nodded. "Yep. They're doughnuts."

The other assembled investigators, inwardly feeling that Kuroiwa ought to apologize to doughnuts everywhere for that assessment, then heard Misato's merciless voice chime in, "Dig in, everybody!"

Later, after all her colleagues save Kuroiwa had fallen ill with a mysterious stomach illness, Misato stared at a photo of her handmade treats. Sure, they didn't look so great, but they'd been prepared with a real homemade touch and lots of love. She thought they'd turned out rather well compared to when she'd first started making treat likes these. Maybe she'd be ready to give some to *him* soon.

Yes, Misato secretly had feelings for someone: up-and-coming Ghoul Investigator Kotaro Amon. He was strong, brave, resolute—the very image of what a Ghoul investigator should be.

Several months earlier, Amon and Misato had fought alongside one another in the Aogiri cleanup operation. She was too nervous to bring herself to speak to him, even though they weren't strangers or anything. She hadn't run into him since then, and now she wanted to take action in order to take their relationship to the next level.

She'd made her treats with that in mind. She'd heard that Amon liked sweet things, and so she'd come up with a plan to give him some homemade doughnuts as a gift.

Her other coworkers had been so happy they'd been moved to tears, so Amon was sure to be happy with them as well. And so, Misato decided to take a break from her professional duties and go see him.

———————

"Investigator Amon? He's not here right now."

Misato had snuck down to the 20th Ward branch office with her doughnuts wrapped up in a cute little bag. Wanting to first find out what Amon was doing, she'd happened upon one of the 20th Ward's more eccentric investigators, Juzo Suzuya, and asked him.

His response, however, was not what Misato had been expecting to hear. "He's not here?"

"No. Mr. Shinohara wanted him for something, I guess? He's out in the 8th Ward now," Juzo said, speaking in his rather unique cadence.

"Oh , I . . . I see. When will he be coming back?"

"When? Hmm . . . I'm not really sure." Juzo rubbed a finger against his forehead and craned his neck. Either he didn't know, or he'd been told and had just forgotten.

How could Amon not be in the 20th Ward? Misato couldn't help but be disappointed. She'd wanted Amon to try her freshly made doughnuts, and she didn't have enough time left today to go to the 8th Ward.

"I see. Well, I guess I don't have much choice," Misato said,

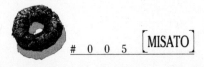

0 0 5 [MISATO]

taking out the doughnuts and handing them to Juzo. "Here's a little something from the 13th Ward, Juzo Suzuya. I hope you'll all enjoy them." She didn't want anyone to know she'd made the doughnuts for Amon, so she invented a quick little lie.

Juzo took the doughnuts, his nose sniffing audibly before he smiled and said, "Maybe I'll go give these to Seidou or something."

Several days later, Misato heard that Seido Takizawa, a rank 2 investigator from the 20th Ward, was out sick due to some health issues, but she couldn't be concerned about that right now.

She'd come to the station near the 8th Ward branch office, where Amon was working temporarily in order to help with a short-age of personnel. Misato checked her map as she headed to the office, taking side streets in order to get there as quickly as possible. Today she'd be sure to give her doughnuts to Amon. Her emotions were running high.

She wasn't prepared for what she ran into en route, however. She gasped. "Th-that's . . ."

It was a man, 191 centimeters tall, with a broad, well-honed frame. There was no mistaking it: there, just up ahead, was Kotaro Amon. Did this chance meeting perhaps mean that fate had bound them together? All at once, Misato's daydreaming went into over-drive, but she came back to reality when she heard Amon speaking to someone.

Looking more closely, she saw a man next to Amon looking back at her curiously, and a woman who appeared to hand something to Amon. Misato's eyes naturally fixed on the woman. *Now just who is that?!*

She pressed herself flat against the wall as if hiding were even an option at this point. The man was still looking right at her, his expression increasingly more perplexed.

The woman was young, fair-skinned, and gorgeous, the kind men went crazy over. And she was talking to Amon.

"You said that you wished the cake I gave you before was sweeter so . . . here."

Wham. The shock hit Misato like a kokaku Quinque blow to the head. This woman had just given Amon one of her homemade cakes. And this wasn't even the first time, apparently. She couldn't get a good look at Amon's face, but she did see him accept the cake, so clearly the prospect didn't bother him much.

Misato's legs began to wobble on the spot. Just what kind of relationship did these two have?

Listening closer, she heard the woman call Amon "Kotaro." Misato's vision went dark.

She could only assume that these two were courting one another before marriage.

"Ngh . . ." Misato turned and ran from the cruel reality before her. She'd just seen their relationship end before it even had a chance to begin. Covering her face to hold back her tears, she bolted through the side streets at a speed befitting a track star.

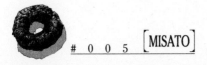

0 0 5 [MISATO]

However, someone came walking around the corner from the station, and Misato plowed right into them, hard enough to bowl the average person clean over.

Apparently they were able to take it, however. "Oof! Whew, you hit me like a shot from a gun right there!" they said, looking down at Misato in astonishment.

It was Taishi Fura, the Ghoul investigator in charge of the 7th Ward. Misato was pretty sure he was currently on the Ghoul restaurant case.

He wasn't alone, however.

"Hey, aren't you that girl who works for Investigator Kuroiwa? Miss Gori, right?"

"Yeah, that's her. What's she doing in a place like this?" It was the ever-itinerant Yanagi and his junior partner, Toujou.

What were these guys doing here? Misato was understandably curious, but she was in no emotional state to have a conversation now. She was certain she'd burst into tears before she got even a single word out.

Still, knowing that she owed them an apology, she took the doughnuts out of the bag. "I'm so sorry!" she said as she pressed them into Fura's hands.

These doughnuts were a gift that could never be given to their intended recipient now. Better that they should eaten by someone than go unappreciated.

Misato bowed her head to the other three investigators, and then ran off again.

II

Misato was down in the dumps after catching sight of Amon's fiancée. She channeled her sadness into her work, and her Ghoul extermination rate went up, but work couldn't fill the hole that was in her heart.

She'd heard that the junior investigators from the 7th Ward had all come down with severe abdominal pains, but their suffering was probably light compared to Misato's own heartbreak.

Amon had been called back to the 20th Ward and was hard at work, she'd heard. Were things going well with him and his girlfriend, she wondered? Was he working so hard in order to make a happy home for the two of them? The more Misato thought of it, the more her emotions ran rampant.

But there was someone who'd noticed how she'd changed.

"Misato?" It was Special Class Investigator Kuroiwa, whom she deeply respected. He called out to her at the end of his shift.

Misato gazed into his bulging eyes, and then hung her head. "Oh, Mr. Kuroiwa, you can see how troubled I've been, can't you?"

"Mm-hmm."

Misato bit her lip hard. "I'm so ashamed of myself, Mr. Kuroiwa. I lost my composure in the face of a fearsome enemy, and I just ran! I'm so powerless!" she wailed, memories of the days she spent working her heart out making doughnuts for Amon flashing through her mind.

Flour scattered about, eggs with the shell mixed in, doughnut

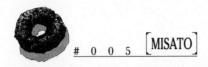

0 0 5 [MISATO]

batter that refused to set no matter how hard she worked it and worked it . . .

A splatter of oil, licks of fire leaping forth from the pan, a kitchen ablaze . . . and then finally, the thing that made it all worth it—her own homemade doughnuts.

She was crying so hard she couldn't speak. Tears actually welled up in her eyes. Kuroiwa looked down at her. "Misato," he called out.

Misato looked up and saw his bulging eyes looking back at her. She stiffened. "Mr. Kuroiwa, you're always telling me not to give up without a fight, not to cry until the battle is done."

"Mm-hmm," Kuroi-wa replied with a nod.

"And that you nev-er know until you try, and to not set limits for yourself, and if you do have limits to just smash right on through them . . ."

"Mm-hmm." Kuroi-wa's tone resounded, stirring the despondent Misato's spirits.

"That someday you'll have to depend on yourself, that the

one thing you should never do is run away, to not let yourself regret things, to take whatever comes your way, to keep moving forward!"

"Mm-hmm," murmured Kuroiwa as he headed off.

Kuroiwa's words resonated in Misato's heart. That's right! Just because her competition was some gorgeous young woman who was probably good at cooking, she wasn't about to give up on her feelings for Amon. The light flared back into Misato's eyes. "I'm going to make some doughnuts and go to the 20th Ward!"

And then, with an invincible fervor, Misato marched right back home to make doughnuts. It was a process she was quite familiar with by now. With a roaring oil fire that barely even scorched the ceiling, she had her doughnuts.

With those in hand, she rushed from the house, headed for the 20th Ward and Kotaro Amon.

But there was something she hadn't considered.

"Inspector Amon's already gone home."

It had taken Misato some time to get home from work, make the doughnuts, and then travel to the 20th Ward branch office. By the time she arrived it was past eight, and Amon had gone home after his shift.

Misato's spirits plummeted from the height of exultation into a pit of despair. "How . . . could this . . . happen . . .?" She dragged herself wearily out of the 20th Ward branch office. Why couldn't things

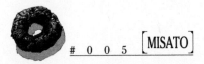

0 0 5 [MISATO]

go well for her? Was there no God?

"Huh?" Misato suddenly heard a gentle voice off somewhere, singing.

She looked to see a young man in front of the 20th Ward train station, somewhere around twenty years old, strumming a guitar and singing. Probably he was a street musician. The tones drew her into the crowd of onlookers, the gentle melody soothing Misato's heart.

God is there, yeah, don't lose sight . . .

As soon as Misato heard those lyrics, tears began to stream from her eyes like tiny waterfalls. The other people listening to the song were quite bewildered as to why someone else in the audience had burst out crying.

More people had turned their attention to her than to the musician by the time a man happened to exit the station, stopping to look at Misato. "Say, haven't I seen you before, miss?"

Misato forcefully wiped away her tears and looked back at this person who'd spoken to her, but she had no idea who he was. She was dubious, but the man then looked up with a burst of recognition on his face. "Oh, that's right! Don't you know Mr. Amon?"

At that, Misato flinched bodily. "Wh-wh-wh . . ."

"You might not remember me, miss, because you were looking at Mr. Amon the whole time. It was on those backstreets in the 8th Ward. I think when Mr. Amon got that little present. I was with him then."

He had to mean when that young woman had given Amon the cake. Misato's memories finally placed the man. He must've been the guy who'd been staring at her in confusion.

"I'm a detective. Name's Morimine. So do you live here in the 20th Ward, miss?"

"No, I . . . I don't, I . . ."

"You don't? Well then what are you doing here? Looks like you've been crying," Morimine said, before stopping short. "Ah," he muttered. "Did something happen with Mr. Amon?" he asked brazenly.

Misato was felt her heart skip a beat, steam nearly about to burst forth from her head. "Ah! N-n-no, I . . ." she stammered, shaking both her hands and her head in denial.

"Mr. Amon strikes me as a bit oblivious," Morimine continued regardless.

"Nothing happened between Kotaro Amon and I! I merely came here to give something to him!"

"I see. And were you able to give it to him?"

Misato couldn't muster up the words to respond.

Morimine regarded her with a sympathetic gaze. "I've got an idea," he suggested. "Why don't you come with me? I'm on my way to see Mr. Amon right now."

"What?! You're going to see Kotaro Amon?!"

"Yep. I made some plans to go out for drinks with him."

It was an opportunity she hadn't dared ask for. But Misato was scared now. What would she do if he wound up not liking the doughnuts?

But then, in the back of her mind, Misato remembered Kuroiwa. His figure, and his kind words. He was right. She couldn't cry until

0 0 5 [MISATO]

the battle was done.

Misato fixed her gaze on Morimine. "Yes, please!" she cried.

They went to a pub that was less than a five-minute walk from the station.

"Oh. Hey! Mr. Amon!" Morimine called out.

Amon had been waiting outside the front door, and he turned to look at Morimine. "Hey there. Sorry to make you come out all this way." He then noticed Misato, standing next to Morimine. "Huh? Gori, from the 13th Ward? What's she doing here?" he asked, eyes wide with surprise.

"Oh, I ran into her over at the train station. She said she had something to give you," Morimine explained. "Well, here he is, miss," he prompted. There was no turning back now.

"Kotaro Amon!"

"Uh . . . yes?"

Misato thrust her hand into her bag and took hold of the wrapped-up doughnuts.

Oh, Investigator Kuroiwa, I've finally come this far. All I have to do now is just hand him the doughnuts. Please, somehow, give me the courage I need, Investigator Kuroiwa! Investigator Kuroiwa . . . Investigator Kuroiwa . . . !

"Investigator Kuroiwaaa! Homemade doughnuts!" She shoved the doughnuts hard against Amon's chest.

"H-homemade?" he stammered in confusion. "Investigator Kuroiwa wanted me to have these?"

"Yes! He told me to give them to you!"

"B-but why?"

"Because you're special, Kotaro Amon!"

"I . . . I'm special? I mean . . . thank you, but . . . why?"

Morimine muttered to himself. "These two aren't on the same page, huh?" But neither Amon nor Misato heard him.

Amon opened the bag to check its contents, the scent of Misato's special doughnuts making him recoil as it hit him all at once. Beads of sweat formed on his forehead. "Uh, these are a bit . . ."

"Investigator Kuroiwa ate them happily enough!" Misato said, jabbing a finger at Amon.

Amon peered inside the bag, drawing his lips back hard. He was thinking. Maybe he wasn't good at handling spicy things, and was trying to get past his own taste preferences?

"All right, Gori. I'll have these all right now!" With that, Amon shoved his hand into the bag, and crammed the contents into his mouth all at once.

"Whoa!" Morimine stiffened, watching from off to the side. Harsh crumbling sounds resounded from Amon's mouth, but rather than hurriedly choking them down, he chewed them up nice and thoroughly before swallowing with an audible gulp.

He then clapped both hands together and bowed his head. "Ah, delicious!" Misato looked on, eyes welling up with deep emotion. It had been a long road, but at long last, she had reached her goal.

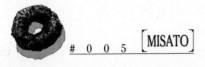

0 0 5 [MISATO]

"Uh, hey? Miss?"

Misato trembled with joy, Morimine's words not even reaching her, and she darted off. Amon had accepted the doughnuts she'd made for him. And he'd eaten every last one right in front of her eyes. She was sure he'd gotten a glimpse of her feminine side. She rushed through the nighttime streets. Oh, she was so, so happy!

Several days later, when she arrived at the 13th Ward office in the morning, Kuroiwa called out to her. "Misato!"

"Yes, what is it?"

"I got a thank-you note from Kotaro Amon from the 20th Ward, but I have no idea what for."

He held out the note, on which had been written, *"Thank you so much for everything."* For a while, the two of them stared at the letter in silence, and then Kuroiwa nodded. "Mm-hmm."

Misato looked a while longer, and then it hit her. "He probably wanted to express his appreciation for some trivial thing you did for him that you didn't even notice. Amon's a very nice young man, wouldn't you say, Investigator Kuroiwa?"

"Mm-hmm."

Amon was a man with a strong sense of duty. He'd surely re-member to thank Misato for the doughnuts she'd given him, too. She nodded back at Kuroiwa, already thinking up what she might make as a gift for Amon next time.

Later that day, a message was sent out from HQ to all branches, telling all staff to be careful about an unexplained stomach illness that had been making its way through the CCG as of late.

TOKYO GHOUL

I'm very happy to get to be part of the *Tokyo Ghoul* world once again.
Thank you to Sui Ishida and to all fans of *Tokyo Ghoul*.

Shin Towada

Glad to be back for round two! I'm very grateful to Shin Towada for responding to this challenge. Once again, thank you very much!

Sui